John White

Peace and other poems

John White

Peace and other poems

ISBN/EAN: 9783337223359

Printed in Europe, USA, Canada, Australia, Japan

Cover: Foto ©Andreas Hilbeck / pixelio.de

More available books at **www.hansebooks.com**

AND OTHER POEMS.

BY

JOHN J. WHITE.

———————

PHILADELPHIA
J. B. LIPPINCOTT & CO.
1867.

v

CONTENTS.

1 *   5

PEACE.

I.

WITH Peace returned, and Reason's even sway
　　Once more resumed within the balanced mind,
Tell, Muse! the cause why, in such dread array,
This age of light and loftier hopes should find
Men armed in deadly conflict with their kind;
Why brethren, in a land so truly free,
Thought, purpose, act, enjoyment unconfined,
Should meet again in hostile rivalry,
As erst, in former years and climes beyond the sea.

II.

Was it for this our fathers crossed the main?
For this they founded, on a distant shore,
New forms of government, where Peace should reign
And shower her choicest blessings evermore?
If such the fruits their labors, sufferings bore,
Alas! for hope upon this dreary earth!
That blissful period, prophesied of yore,
The long millenial reign, the rule of worth,
When nations shall not war, will never know a birth.

7

III.

I dreamed in youth there was one model state,
And that my country,—where the social tie
Bound first the family; and Virtue sate
Enthroned throughout its ruling polity:
That polity so framed that scarce was I
Aware of its existence, but to bless:—
Yet blessing as it did, it felt not nigh,
Nor ruffled o'er the tranquil consciousness,
That, for its rule, my joys, my means were nought the less.

IV.

Methought that discord never might be raised
Within that commonwealth, my place of birth,—
A land for institutions justly praised,
As pioneer of gentler days on earth:—
Nor, in its union with the kindred worth
Of states around it in a nation's name,
Did jealous Freedom fear her sacred hearth
Endangered, in its pure and heavenly flame,
By lust for·power, or pomp, or wealth, or dearer fame.

V.

Removed afar, upon its virgin soil
Of boundless scope and wild luxuriance,
From pent up crowds who, never ceasing, toil
To wrest a stinted dole from doubtful chance,
And daily gain their bare deliverance
Of life itself—our easy, healthful task
Served, as the Spartan sauce, but to enhance
The zest for Nature's richest gifts—to ask
Was to receive,—enjoy,—and in her bounties bask.

VI.

Not in the treasures of the teeming land,
The matchless wealth of vast primeval woods,
The promised gains upon her ocean strand,
Nor lesser promise of her inland floods,—
Those seas innumerous, whose varied moods
Of storm and calm oft task the pilot's skill,
Nor wastes of mineral wealth, where none intrudes
Save but to sound their richness,—hath her fill
Of blessings poured from land, and lake, and strand, and hill.

VII.

All these were hers—and much that poets feigned,
Or eastern dreamers, wild in wondrous lore,— '
Yet least were they of what our fathers gained,
As pious pilgrims to this western shore:
A world were little to that priceless store
Of moral wealth displayed to erring men,—
A conquest grander than e'er made before,
Throughout earth's blood-stained hist'ry's tablet, when
Her wildest savage bowed, the enduring friend of Penn.

VIII.

He sought not theirs, but them,—(as they who seek,
Clothed with their measure of th' Apostle's love,
That heirship promised only to the meek*),—
And gained them, girt with armor from above:
All power was his those fiercest souls to move,
In Christlike self-devotion to their weal;
And they and theirs have never failed to prove
How firm that bond, which bore nor oath, nor seal,
Has held in friendship fast, as 'twere with hooks of steel.

* Matt. v. 5.

IX.

Oh! most auspicious settlement! the ground
Of blessings seldom felt by man before;
And loving hearts this novel compact wound
In ties of bliss on Pennsylvania's shore;
So like a paradise her regions o'er,
So much the famed Arcadia poets feign,
That love and peace. not hatred, lust, and war,
Near four-score years held undisputed reign,
And nations saw, amazed, an Eden come again.

X.

Yet small, in sooth, that promise to the hope
Of mingling contrasts in their wide extreme;
For rarely met beneath celestial cope,
A group of men the sagest mind could deem
Less fitted for the famed Utopian dream
Of harmony—the blood-stained victor's son,[1]—
Trained in that school, whose logic would esteem
All title vested in th' imperial throne,
To grant barbarian lands discovery had won.

XI.

And there the savage in his woodland home,
Which white men had invaded, and by fraud
Made captives of their swarthy tribes who roam,
For horrid fate in unknown climes abroad;[2]
(What wonder if our race should be outlawed
By such fell deeds!)—the savage, foremost bred
To bear, inflict, and, merciless, applaud
The strongest nerve in both,—tortures more dread
Than Inquisition heaped on Israelitish head.

XII.

How little recked the monarch, in his grant
Of lands where mighty commonwealths would be,
If justice gave him sceptred power to plant
Aggressive colonies beyond the sea;
How little cared he for the native, free,
Time-honored denizens who trod the soil;
From the Great Spirit's gift they claimed their fee,
He his through papal fiction; but the moil
Of war must arbitrate, the victor seize the spoil.

XIII.

Such, as his right, he gave,—and sovereign law,
In christian realms, forbade all useless doubt;
Too soon, by acts, the simple native saw
His swift impending ruin brought about
From fraud to force, and force to fatal rout,
Till, maddened with increasing wrongs, he rose
In union's strength to drive these tyrants out,
Nor sex nor age distinguished in his foes,
Nor dealt by rule and courtesy his murd'rous blows.

XIV.

Justice and Mercy! there they met on earth,—
Twain, yet one pillar of th' eternal Throne;
So like in consequence, so near in birth,
That He, the visible, the incarnate Son,
Could but in practice blend them into one,
As judge, enforced, of crime,—to sin no more,*
His heaviest sentence for a deed begun,
Man, unregenerate, pardoned ne'er before,[3]
But washed its blackness out with seas of human gore.

* John viii. 11.

XV.

There sat the painted savage,—there the sage,
And christian stood 'neath Shackamaxon's tree;
How grand the theme! though in that passing age
Few felt the era; none, perchance, but he
The crisis reached for human liberty;
Simple the words,—though simple, yet sincere,—
Sincerity then joined with purity,—
These the two wings, the angel wings that bear [1]
The soul, redeemed from earth, to reach its heavenly sphere.

XVI.

Penn's eye was single; his unclouded sight
Fixed on the moral source of perfect day;
The body filled with more than solar light,*
And clear and plain the one unchanging way,—
To do to others as he would that they
Should do in turn to him ; that little stone,†
Cut from the mountain without hands, that lay
In dust man's image, Policy, o'erthrown,—
The gold, the clay, the brass, all mingled into one.

XVII.

And, as we read, that stone a mountain grew,‡
And filled the earth,—so, small howe'er their start,
Successive treaties recognized the due
Thus given the red man,—and the spoiler's art,
Which Rome and Spain had grafted on the chart
Of Europe's claim to heathen lands, destroyed,[5]
The christian might, consistently, impart
Christ's precepts to the savage, unannoyed
By taunt for deeds that made his lofty teachings void.

---

* Matt. vi. 22.　　　† Matt. vii. 12.　　　‡ Daniel ii. 35.

XVIII.

Nor circumscribed to this that righteous act,—
In blessing he was blest, and all were blest;
Virtues are boon companions,—they attract
Each heavenly attribute their welcome guest,
And one is ever sample of the rest;
The good man and the wise are never twain;
He ranks the greatest who is found the best:
Like stars reflected on the quivering main,
Their glowing traits of love repeat themselves again.

XIX.

Need we then marvel that, from such a dawn,
In peace and splendor rose the glorious day,
More perfect than the eye had looked upon,
With moral light and pure religion's ray?
Beneath that just, and wise, and gentle sway,
Conscience achieved its freedom from the chains[6]
Of human law, and each his several way
Might worship God, secure from corp'ral pains
Imposed by bigot fools where Superstition reigns.

XX.

This grand foundation deeply, firmly laid,
The only rock for christian commonwealth;
Wise legislation gave its genial aid
To build a system for the future health
Of millions, and the corresponding wealth
Which vast communities might owe to law;
Simple at first and, as it were, by stealth
Before the age, our Solon's eye foresaw
That such the worthiest sons of Europe's soil would draw.

2

XXI.

How great his forecast, e'en in pettier things,
Let this his Philadelphia's growth attest!
Would that its shore, whose crowded margin brings
The pestilence a not unfrequent guest,
Were, as he willed, in beauteous verdure drest!
But mammon's touch hath made it otherwise,
And sties and filth its former sward infest;
The mart whence noisome odors ever rise,
Where he had left a bank of green declivities.[7]

XXII.

Within two centuries huge forests stood,
And he, the founder, here with finished plan,
More than developed now; the mazy wood
Hath long since passed away,—the mightier man
Behold around! where wealth, where progress span,
For use and beauty, earth, o'er plain and hill;
Yet these his least memorials,—he began
As wisest architect,—the principle
Of each and all then laid for Time but to fulfil.

XXIII.

The germs were there of this prodigious fruit,—
The frame of what we since have realized;[8]
God, only, sovereign lord of conscience,—mute
On this the empires scheming men devised,
Since priestly craft hath held the power it prized;
Coeval fraud and force. and wile and war,
Twin brood which, loss of human prey surmised,
Dark, baleful Superstition trains to mar
The truth, and from its light th' imprisoned spirit bar.

XXIV.

The church, in her hands such colossal power,
Engine most monstrous of the selfish few,
Regained with him the beauty of that hour,
When two or three were met in worship true;*
Those whom allegiance to their Master drew,
With humble faith and childlike confidence,
Their strength in meekness, silence to renew,
Save when He bade it broken,—nor pretence
Was there of outward aid to please each carnal sense.

XXV.

God is a spirit,—they that worship him,†
Must worship him in spirit and in truth:—
How fain would grovelling wisdom seek to dim
This, which was proved e'er Time's corroding tooth
Had 'gan to ravage Eden's blooming youth;—
When, as we learn, He moved upon its face,
Earth without form, to change the gloom uncouth,
Of chaos dark to heavenly ordered grace,
And man, his temple, there in innocence to place.

XXVI.

That temple still are they, who, like the king,‡
Israel's sweet psalmist, would a house essay
To build, as all are bidden, and to bring
Thither to hearts sincere his perfect sway;
With such who thus receive Him, in his way
Of coming, He will sup, and ever dwell,§—
Cimmerian darkness yield to brightest day,
And man, redeemed, as sacred penmen tell,
Shall reach that former peace in God from whence he fell.

* Matt. xviii. 20.   † John iv. 24.   ‡ 1 Cor. iii. 16.   § Rev. iii. 20.

XXVII.

Contrast we then the early infant state,
On this foundation broadly, deeply laid,
With the great nation, self-convulsed so late
In civil war—they differ most in grade,—
Save where prosperity and strength have made,
With time and circumstance and worldly gain,
As erst the church, its primal bloom to fade,
Corrupted by success,—and proud and vain,
Its virtue yield to vice—wisdom to folly's reign.

XXVIII.

Nor church nor priestly power may claim, by law,
O'er human conscience more that dread control,[9]
Maintained in blood and crime, when Europe saw
Her worthiest brave the stormy ocean's roll,
The unknown, howling wilderness their goal :—
But yet, alas! encroachment hath begun
Its secret web to snare again the soul,—
Softly—yet surely onward—one by one
The yielding barriers prove how strong the net that's spun.[10]

XXIX.

Encroachment, too, hath blurred the goodliest frame,
Which wisdom, virtue, circumstance combined,
Enabled men to form and truly name,
A self-sustaining rule of human kind;
But checks, and balances, and powers assigned,
With functions, duties, rights, in language clear.
Are cobwebs in their path, when factions blind,
Impelled at first by lust, at last by fear
Distrust and hate, sweep on in folly's mad career.

XXX.

Who "take the sword shall perish with the sword :"
From heaven no more immutable decree;—
If single champions learn that skill abhorred,
To pierce a brother's breast in victory,
Soon may their own the fatal target be :—
So with the nation's course,—if trust in arms
Divert its strength to martial rivalry,
'Tis but to rouse, in turn, with dire alarms,
Like strength and jealous fears, which bring war's dreaded
    storms.

XXXI.

What boots our hatred, fierce as Rome displayed
When Brutus freed her, to the name of king,
If regal rule, in other forms arrayed,
All of its ills, except the pageant, bring!
Was Cæsar's laurel less the direful spring
Of more than Tarquin's tyranny and lust?
Did Marius, the plebeian leader, fling
O'er outraged Law a higher, holier trust,
When, with the people's will, he trailed it in the dust!

XXXII.

Survey the course of commonwealths and states;
Those which may most th' heroic age recall :—
Behold them in their phases and their fates!
How like they start, they culminate, and fall,
The prey at last of military thrall,
That stern resource to save society :
Does not the mystic writing on the wall,
The Past—show what the Future yet will be,
That Venice, Greece, Rome, France, may type our destiny?

2 *   B

XXXIII.

Or, turning to cotemporary deeds,
And kindred polities upon our shore,—
Who, in the constant strife of factions, reads[11]
Bright promise for a country, yet in store,
So deeply bathed in fratricidal gore,—
So lately to its whole foundation shaken,—
Must, like Napoleon, hear in battle's roar
Freedom's all hail! and not her knell, awaken:—
Delusive thought! 'tis such her soul has most forsaken.

XXXIV.

The home of Freedom is alone with Law;—
An axiom—e'en if tyrants legislate:—
Law, fixed and certain, whose behests withdraw
From party, passion, weakness, and from hate,
Our rights and wrongs when on its turn they wait:—
How infinitely so where none may claim,
Beyond his fellow, influence in the state,
More than is justly due an honored name,
His wisdom, genius, wealth, or right to nobler fame.

XXXV.

Such have we deemed this exquisitely wrought,
And wisely fitting, complicated plan,—
Embodiment of all that human thought
And learning, since society began,
Have framed, to steady frail and erring man—
Can it be such when huge, gigantic war,
Like wild and all devouring fire, hath ran,
Throughout its length and breadth, the country o'er,
Till every hamlet's hearth the pall of mourning wore!

XXXVI.

Can we affirm the mighty problem solved,
Of human government? which, erst, our sires,
From schemes and theories with doubt involved,
Essayed to find in this—whose aim aspires
To reach the loftiest pitch of man's desires:
This was the grand experiment,—the test
Is made and ended in war's fiercest fires:
Law failed—the wage of battle, as the best,
Has proved its mazy plan defective like the rest.

XXXVII.

How feeble wisest checks and guards, to stay
The selfish greed of men, or Passion's course!
Oh! may what here commenced in Virtue's sway,
Ne'er know dependence on the law of force,
The dread precursor of that last resource,
Despotic rule, for refuge from the hot,
Blind fury of the multitude,—that curse
Of states, the scourge of faction—such the lot
Of all who wisdom's ways and self-control forgot.

XXXVIII.

What though the conquering sword has brought us peace,
And awed the nations with display of power,—
Will wars and rumors, through its action, cease?
Alas! e'en now portentous warnings lower
Along the sky, as if this crimson dower
Were fastened surely on the hapless strand:
Wherefore the joy for fierce, triumphant hour
Of conquest, if the sabre must command
Obedience, and a change hath passed across the land!

XXXIX.

Shall we yet sigh, and, henceforth, sigh in vain,
As memory wanders to those blissful days,
When, through each state, Law's unimpeded reign,
By moral force, would draw the stranger's praise
At scenes so foreign to his country's ways :[12]—
When, in its several orbit, each was moved
Around the central sun—whose genial rays,
With heat and light, attraction ample proved
To bring e'en distant stars within a sphere so loved.

XL.

Such was of power our balance—such the fruit;—
Not, as in Europe, with its legions armed,—
Each country sensitive to every bruit,—
By every change, or chance in strength, alarmed;
Our cheap defence of nations, while it warmed
To stronger life within, around it drew
New clustered commonwealths—and, swiftly swarmed,
Came rushing crowds, who in its bosom grew,
Transformed in all but birth,—the old world to the new.

XLI.

Oh! rich reality of every hope!
More bright than Plato's, Locke's, or Sidney's scheme!
Our progress distanced e'en the airy scope
Of Fancy's picture in her wildest dream;
What lacked, to change the yet empurpled stream
Of future hist'ry to a flow of peace;
The cannon's roar, the dreaded bay'net's gleam,
No more offending—war and strife to cease,
And man intent alone on Virtue's wide increase?

XLII.

For this was he created,—Eden knew
Its sole director Him who, styled as love
By one that nearest to his presence grew,
And, longest living, most essayed to prove
This attribute, was emblemed by the dove :—
In teaching, suffering, acts, th' incarnate Son
No other aid revealed, to point above
The aspirations of a race undone :—
By this, alone, could be the heavenly kingdom won.

XLIII.

Brute force the heathen's staff hath ever been,—
Too oft the self-styled christian's—but the way,
Taught and displayed by all that man had seen
Of Christ himself, was marked in Virtue's sway ;—
In moral strength Penn's wondrous secret lay—
Th' eternal power of justice and of truth :—
Transmitted, though diffused, its kindling ray
Illumed this Union in its glorious youth,—
Begrimed and mangled now by War's ensanguined tooth.

XLIV.

Christ's advent was in peace, good-will to men :—
Our founders built on this as on a rock ;
No longer earth that huge afflicted den
Of spoilers, ravaging its weaker flock,
But brethren of one race and kindred stock ;
From oaths, from priestly rule the conscience free,
Their patient labors tended to unlock
The prison-house of ages,—would that we,
In life, and faith, and works, could their successors be !

XLV.

Christ's kingdom, not of this world, wins by love;—
Cæsar's, opposed, through force, impelled by lust :*
The first with self-denial seeks to prove
A heavenly origin in truth and trust,
Though often trailed its banner in the dust,
Despised and outlawed—yet anew to rise,
More glorious from the ignominy thrust
On it as on its Master,—to the skies,
Borne on the wings of joy with heavenly harmonies.

XLVI.

Far other of this world the baleful sway!
The Roman typed it, and the Greek still more†—
Through Asia's blood and tears who cut his way
In aimless rage to distant India's shore,
And wept for other worlds to ravage o'er,—
Glutted and gorged with slaughter, then who turned
A scorpion on himself—the battle's roar
Fit prelude to debauch—and him, who spurned
All human rights and fears, the drunkard's grave inurned.

XLVII.

His the mere lust to conquer—dare we give
The christian's praise to higher motived war?
Will he, who takes another's life, receive
The answer of "well done!" before that bar,
The one which finds us truly what we are?
He, the great Judge, hath bade his followers love
E'en those who hate them,—stronger reason far
That such as hate us not should feelings move
To meet, as meet they ought who claim one Sire above.

* James iv. 1, 2.   † Alexander.

XLVIII.

Immortal spirits—who, confessed, are here
Placed for an endless being to prepare,—
And rise from sin's dark region to a sphere
Of infinite enjoyment—or to bear
Its natal curse beyond the reach of prayer:—
Can they be doomed, worse than the beasts of prey,
To rouse all passions, and all crimes to share,
Produce all horrors—light their lurid way
With deeds that make such brutes fiends less by far than they?

XLIX.

For this is War!—no tongue nor pen may trace
The cruelties,—the sufferings,—ruin, brought
O'er earth's fair regions, where its hours efface
The years of industry—its scorchings blot
All joy and beauty from the goodliest spot:
It moves but to destroy—and greater now
The havoc science, skill, and means have wrought
To pile th' enormous mound of human wo,
Too like before of scenes we dreamed of hell below.

L.

When erst in combat men with men engaged,
Their weapons rude, such war as Homer sang,—
With strength—with prowess,—hand to hand 'twas waged,
And death itself seemed robbed of many a pang;
When fiercest passions from their efforts sprang,
Excitement blunted much the awful game;—
But chivalry, whose arms on armor rang,
Hath yielded long to modes more swift and tame,
To unseen crashing bolts from distant sheets of flame.

LI.

In colder blood proceeds the work of doom :—
A mere automaton the soldier stands,
Obedient—silent—till his vacant room,
By viewless missile made from unknown hands,
The close of column o'er his form demands :—
Poor wretch! too oft to linger out, of life,
His hours or days on desolated strands,—
What thoughts are his, apart from child, or wife.
Or home, of dread account, fresh from fraternal strife !

LII.

Men merely emulate their kindred brutes
In single slaughters,—but the boundless mind
Brings science to its service, and the fruits,
For Death's grim harvest, sweep the sulph'rous wind
In hundred folds more fatal to mankind,—
One petty combat changed all naval war.*
And the world's fleets to desuetude consigned :
Since then the iron walls, increased, but bar
Attack till heavier bolt of steel the turret jar.

LIII.

Shall we, indeed, the fable yet enact,
Which poets feigned, of Titans with the gods,
Or Milton's fancied fight reduce to fact?
What were the rocks, the hugest mountain clods,
To bombs which burst in fragments man's abodes !
What spears of pine trees whole to tons of steel
Hurled on with lightning speed across the floods,
To crush the fort or make the iron-clad reel !
Sunk with her living freight e'er ceased the echoing peal !

* Between the Monitor and Merrimac.

LIV.

So fast for death the awful progress made,
That few can follow swift destruction's ways;—
Each month—each week—some fresh foundation laid
To rouse our jealous fear of evil days,
When hostile engines suddenly may raze
Our cities to the earth—for such a change
In nations passes like a meteor's blaze
Across heaven's arch—witness the fatal range
Of Prussia's gun,—results in war nor new nor strange.

LV.

Her laurels vanished in as brief a space
On Jena's bloody field,—and there a power
Now highest, e'er then highest, bowed its face,
Deep humbled in the dust—the mighty dower
That Frederic gave her gone within an hour;—
Such fortune may ere long be her's again:—
O'er startled Europe clouds begin to lower,
Whose dark portentous folds may drench the plain,
For war breeds war—and soon her vast resources drain.

LVI.

No limit then to internecine strife,
Nor bounds to slaughter through its growing means;—
Alike in civil as in savage life,
The constant round of legal murder's scenes,
And short the blessed pause that intervenes:—
Perversely obstinate if cause there be,
And swift to seek it out when interest leans
To quarrel, man is now, though learned and free,
As much as e'er the slave of war's dark rivalry.

LVII.

False honor, in the many as in one,
Pricks on alike to bathe the hands in blood;—
False glory urges—meekness bids to shun
Revenge and hatred with their demon brood,
Opposed to all that's pure and wise and good;
False reason claims the soul and spreads the snare:—
'Tis country calls to hostile attitude!
Her fiat makes Christ's distant brethren wear
A foeman's livery—pledged unceasing hate to bear.

LVIII.

Can human laws convert me to a tool,
Bound and commissioned all my powers, to slay
Those whom the few or many, bearing rule,
Stamp enemies in war?—must I obey,[13]
Or follow Him, the true, eternal way,
And love them—feed them?—such the will of Heaven,
By kindness to o'ercome in christian fray:—
The only one wherein all power is given
To bring lost Eden back, whence man's misrule was driven.

LIX.

Thy empire, Britain! reaches round the globe;
Alarum drums of thine attend the sun;
Thy flag, thy meteor flag, seems as a robe,
Engirdling earth with an unbroken zone,
Where Law transforms the millions into one;
A petty trespass—nay, a less than wrong,
May arm them all war's dreadful course to run;[14]—
Nor singly thus to thee such traits belong,
They find their place alike with nations weak and strong.

LX.

The right thou claim'st—but, when Napoleon's power
Had marshalled Europe's strength to conquer thee,—
When skies were dark, and clouds began to lower
With threatening aspect, then 'twas tyranny,
And thou the self-styled champion of the free!
Enough doth Nemesis return thee now,
Thy poisoned chalice o'er that narrow sea,
In doubts and grounded fears—which ceaseless grow,
While, with his might, his crown is on th' avenger's brow.

LXI.

Thus ever runs the cycle,—years of wrong
Produce their sequence sure in days of fear;
Strength is not all the heirloom of the strong,
And more descends from weakness than the tear;
'Tis thus that law of compensation here
Makes, in the main, an even checkered scene;
Though men may bask in glory's proud career,
And shift its woes on thousands,—it hath been
The nation's lot to know alternate cloud and sheen.

LXII.

If country thus my body claim, and soul,
Despite Christ's plain, consistent, strong command,
I, like the Persian, may refuse control[15]
And waive protection—though possessions stand
A tempting treasure for the ruffian's hand;—
We hold that foreign subjects can annul
Allegiance, and at Europe's hands demand,
As citizens with us, their rights in full:—
We scout their antique laws derived from feudal rule.

LXIII.

Oh! subtle reasoning—such rebellion, late,
Nursed into action—and the flag defied
Which symboled power and unity and state;—
Logic might prove, and irony deride,
But insult touched a nation in its pride;
Laws, amid arms, are silent—vainly strove
The best to soothe—the wisest to decide:
Weak hope! when wildest passions fiercely move
To tame the human heart by reason or by love.

LXIV.

But what is country? is 't my spot of birth,
The rule which governed on my natal day?
Full swiftly rushes change across the earth,
And empires then in flower have passed away:
The names remain—the systems, forms, and sway,
Successful parties long have overthrown:—
Some more, some less, but all have been the prey
Of war and waste—and under burdens groan,
Which grind the peasant's face, to gild the rich alone.

LXV.

Republics rose upon this western world,—
Rebellious colonies, as once was ours,—
Successful treason freedom's flag unfurled,
And carved their right to rank with other Powers;
All have been Faction's sport—as yet there lowers
O'er some the lurid cloud of civil strife;—
Oppressed with every change, the subject cowers
In daily fear for property and life,
For commerce—travel—home—where gleams the bandit's
knife.

LXVI.

I would not check the patriot's ardent zeal,
The love for country—but the christian's aim
Must ever tend to make his brethren feel
That love divine—the heavenly kindled flame,—
Which warms to all God's heritage the same :—
Which bounds cannot divide—nor distance cool—
Our measure of the spirit, He, who came
To save lost sinners, promised us,—to rule
O'er all that springs from earth, or grows in Nature's school.

LXVII.

Shall then a line, that forms thy country's bound,
Force thee to hate thy neighbor and to slay?
Or worse, if factions in that land be found
Imposing—equal—and, in dire array,
Demanding service for their mortal fray,—
No halt allowed thee, and no doubtful mean—
But one thou must oppose, and one obey.—
Can the mere chance of lot on either scene
Compel the deadliest hate where friendship most hath been?

LXVIII.

Each party claims the law, and calls to God,
As erst in battle's wage, for victory :[16]—
Has ever banded army wavering stood
'Twixt right and wrong, as seeming dubiously
To weigh its cause? the strong machinery
Of war whirls swiftly forward to its goal :—
The priest in prayer, the bard in song, agree,
To fan the roaring flames which onward roll,
The motto, Justice—Right—but Passion sweeps the soul.

3 *

LXIX.

Turn we then meekly to the lip of Truth;—
He bids to render Cæsar Cæsar's due,
Obedience—honor—deference—save, in sooth,
When such would make the Truth himself untrue,
Withholding his from God:—nor curious, through
These worldly strifes for power, to scan each cause:
The rex de facto doctrine may anew
Guide through the tangled web allegiance draws;
Though rose be white or red, not ours to brave the laws.[17]

LXX.

Live we within, but not of Cæsar's world:
In simple honesty obey his rule,
The powers above us set—the flag unfurled,
Symbol of sovereign claim,—but in his school
Of fraud, and force, and vice, to stand a fool,
Our highest wisdom and our chiefest good;
We cannot serve our God and be his tool,
Whether his syren's song, or pleasures lewd,
May tempt—or brighter fame—or glory drenched in blood.

LXXI.

His course is often ill, that good may come,—
His weapon war, to bring return of peace;
Such were not theirs who fell in martyrdom,
That scheming fraud and violence might cease,
Right, justice, mercy, truth, and love, increase:—
Nor is Christ's kingdom of this lower sphere,*
Else had his servants fought to gain new lease
Of life and liberty—to hold him here,
For whom they bartered all—than life and all more dear.

* John xviii. 36.

LXXII.

"If," said the Jews, "we let this man alone,
Thus preaching meekness—all will soon believe:—
The Romans come,—our place and nation gone:*
To save his life shall then a people grieve?
Expedient 'tis he die, lest we receive,
As unresisting sheep, the conqueror's chains:—
To arms! the laurelled wreath of victory weave!
The strength of Saul—of David—yet remains,—
And God will march with fire before his chosen trains."

LXXIII.

Vain sophists! strength full oft in weakness lies:
Better, by far, your strength in conscious right!
'Twas more than David in that humble guise
Your madness doomed,—but yours the fatal blight;
The Romans came—and sunk in endless night
Your nation,—razed your Zion to the dust:—
No stone of that proud temple meets the sight;—
Your scattered children, victims to the lust
Of power, still yearn to build with an unfalt'ring trust.

LXXIV.

Long centuries of wo have not effaced
That blindly cherished faith to see again
Their holy city, as she once was graced,
When Sheba crossed Arabia's burning plain
To greet the glories of their wisest's reign;
And more—Messiah yet his sceptre sway,
With majesty, in some resplendent fane,
As gorgeous as the rest—and in that day
All nations, kindreds, tongues, shall his behests obey.

* John xi. 48.

LXXV.

Still outward! still the same; "oh! fools and blind!"
The sharp rebuke to those who vainly sought,
The fruit discarding, in its husk to find
The soul-sustaining nourishment—that brought
Eternal life,—nor all the wonders wrought,
Could change, of pride and hate, their stony heart:
Have we, *their* heathen, inspiration caught
From Truth itself to choose that better part,
Which meekly treads its path and scorns deceptive art?

LXXVI.

Have we the strength, in conscious virtue bold,
At Israel's remnant first to cast the stone,—
Our rule that sinless life—and as, unrolled,
We ponder o'er his precepts one by one,
How stands the record which to Him has gone?
Will He, the final Judge of quick and dead,
Reverse those words upon his awful throne?
Restore bleak Sinai's barren law instead—
And falsify the truth of all he did and said!

LXXVII.

The formal Christian and the outward Jew
Reject alike,—the one with greater shame,—
As he who promises and fails to do
His duty,—merits still severer blame :—
They both deny that ever living name
Made manifest in flesh to erring man:
The inward Jew and Christian—each the same—
See Him—have seen Him—whom, since earth began,
All mortal eyes, ears, senses, thoughts, have failed to scan.

LXXVIII.

When, with his worldly load, the young man sought *
That unknown pathway to eternal life,—
The rule inflexible was simply taught,
To offer all for all—his riches, rife
With seeds of envy, hatred, lust, and strife,
To gain a boundless treasure in the skies;
Such the demand of him who held the knife,
Prompt on Moriah's mount, to sacrifice
The darling of his heart—in faith that he would rise.†

LXXIX.

Such are the terms set forth in that evangel,
The last, the best, from him whom Jesus loved,—
The book more like of some recording angel
Than aught that ever human hearts hath moved;
And coldly skeptic his who ne'er has proved
The quickening touches of its hallowed fire:
Such that new birth in spirit it behooved
All men to undergo, whose hopes aspire
To enter in that realm where rules th' eternal Sire.

LXXX.

And this is Faith,—not in some outward creed,—
But faith in God, omnipotent and good,—
Who, ever present, dwells in very deed,
Whether in crowds or desert solitude,
With those whose secret soul is thus imbued;
Such, as in Eden, seek his sovereign will,—
To do it meekly all their daily food :—
Their lives reflecting, both in good and ill,
That light from Him whose power doth all creation fill.

* Matt. xix. 20. † Heb. xi. 19.

C

LXXXI.

To such, the pilgrims through this fleeting world,
A transitory stage to endless bliss,—
The jar of, warring empires rudely hurled
To ruin, or the chill of faction's hiss,
Will bring less pain than their own deeds amiss:
What matters to the faithful, when the cross
The crown procures in higher spheres than this,—
When countless gain rewards a moment's loss,
What matters fame, or life, or earth with all its dross!

LXXXII.

These truths—these saving truths, who dare deny,
Unless the skeptic—styled of yore the fool,
Who in his heart, by acts, proclaimed the lie,
"There is no God!"—and yet the worldly school,
Whose teachings, counsel, purpose, sternly rule,
Ignore plain words,—command our mutual slaughter,—
Make man, immortal, but a murd'rous tool,
Whose blood, with mingled tears, must flow like water!—
Of Satan's crime this fruit with Sin his fiendlike daughter!

LXXXIII.

How then shall nations act? by suffering wrong,
Invite aggression—further injury?
Must they complacently behold the strong
Increase in strength, and unsuspecting lie,
Till danger rouse inglorious apathy;—
Then, when too late for safety, wake to find
The crushing phalanx of destruction nigh,—
Themselves, like Samson, shorn and doomed to grind,—
Helpless and hopeless slaves—the scorn of all their kind?

LXXXIV.

Let hist'ry answer with her tomes of glory,—
That ceaseless record of recurring war :—
Select as sample aught :—it tells the story,
Pregnant with deep instruction,—just how far
One bloody era serves the next to bar :
Scan the uprising of imperial France,
And trace, till paled the first Napoleon's star,
That round of crime—which, were it wild romance,
Would rank the loftiest sketch of Death's infernal dance.

LXXXV.

As wave on wave,—and each succeeding crest
Falling to rise, and rising but to fall,—
As aimless—armies sprang, and, like the rest
Before them, sank beneath that awful pall,—
The long eclipse which Europe saw enthrall
Her energies for twenty years of strife ;—
The Bourbon came, returned in blood,—but all
The throes—the agonies—the waste of life,
Left nations not the less with vast oppression rife.

LXXXVI.

Again the cycle runs !—Napoleon reigns !—
What progress in stability for peace?
An able despot now, what hope remains
For tranquil ruling law with his surcease?
Will votes unanimous—will vast increase
Of wealth and power secure his dynasty?
Or shall the empire prove another lease
For life or years—another deluge be[18]
Reserved, to burst again from dread futurity?

LXXXVII.

Alas! how small the mote in Europe's eye
To carp at, when the beam is in our own!—
Her varied scenes of mutability
Revolve in circles round one central throne,
And parties change,—while that remains alone
A fixed, unmoving point,—such England's lot:
Her centuries of freedom sparsely sown
With revolutions—nor in these were wrought
More than the Law's defence to bigot sovereigns brought.

LXXXVIII.

That Law supreme—unwritten, but more sure,
In dealing justice than the wisest codes:—
Its vast repertories of thought enure
To check, of fashion's sweep, the swift inroads
Which root up landmarks;—ancient though the modes,
Yet plastic to receive all clear reform;—
If slow, 'tis safe—if burdened with the loads
Of rubbish Time hath brought, 'twill stand the storm
Of Passion, and the shocks of Faction's rage disarm.

LXXXIX.

'Twere well, my country! wert thou thus as she:—
Hadst thou kept firm that bulwark of the state,
The seat of judgment—and in purity
Preserved the snowy robe, no fitting mate
For the low venal motives which await
Him, who to power or popular applause
Must look for doubtful fortune or his fate:
Hadst thou that reverence, worthily, which draws
Its proud respect from those, the guardians of thy laws,

XC.

Then had thy future promise of success:
Oh! for a Mansfield's or a Marshall's day,
Who stood serenely equable, nor less
Impartial, incorrupt, for faction's bray:
To human weakness justice falls a prey,
Unless from tempters—passions—far removed;
From these no care too great to fence the way:
We here have felt how much it thus behooved
To guard from every ill—to foster worth beloved.[19]

XCI.

Yet, fatal error! this is party's spoil,—
And worse—too oft the sport of party change:—
The ermine worth, integrity, should coil,
Selected purely through the widest range,
Then, spotless, kept from all that may estrange
Weak, erring man in sternest duty's path:—
Dependence, fear, or favor may derange
Full many a balanced mind, where Learning hath
Her favored seat—which else would stem the tide of wrath.

XCII.

But with us all is swallowed in the whirl,—
As each Olympiad its game renews;[20]—
The contest closed, again their flags unfurl
In ceaseless struggle—and the crowds who lose,
At once new vigor for their next infuse:
Its hundred thousand offices the prize
Of him, whom best drilled partizans may choose
As chief, to guide the nation's destinies:
And then for each, in troops, the hungry claimants rise.

4

XCIII.

Small is the heed of what their claims may lack,
If party services have made them bold;
The sovereign rule to each succeeding pack,
With added strength—at least for them—must hold:
Rotation is that rule—nor thought of old
Time-honored saws about the public good:—
Our laws of progress scout them, and unfold
How well may serve a fresh and idle brood,—
Do better work, waste less, and please the multitude.

XCIV.

"For forms of government let fools contest,"
Mere folly if the life shall not agree;
"Whate'er is best administered is best;"
And worst the rule where only forms are free:
Will boundless suffrage bring back liberty
With settled laws and universal good,
Or keep obscure that aristocracy
Which nature formed—with mind, with worth endued,
Who shun the vulgar lists where demagogues intrude?

XCV.

Freemen should choose—not slaves to venal lust:
The truth should make them—that alone can free:—
They who have proved their worth are those to trust,
And, trusted—tried—their cultured skill should be,
As in all meaner crafts, the guarantee
Of more and better service—were it so,
That party strife, with furious rivalry,
Would ne'er have been—nor state to state a foe,
Pitted, in mortal hate, to deal its deadliest blow.

XCVI.

'Tis wisdom to confess our faults, and learn;
Such quarrels prove that each hath right and wrong:
Will millions stake their all, and madly spurn
Blessings and gifts, earth's choicest boons among,
Without a cause—aye!—grievances—and strong?[21]
And do we not our polity arraign,
So proved and praised, if errors, sins belong
Not to ourselves—thus arrogant and vain,
To claim that perfect state few mortals may attain?

XCVII.

No form of government so much as ours,
Rests on the love of each—his full consent:
From this its strength:—its delegated powers,
Through legal means, and sparingly, are lent,
And only not abused where all, content,
Should feel that what just rule may give, is given:—
Protection, freedom. in his lawful bent
To move, untrammeled, till life's closing even,
And make, as Eden made it, harbinger of heaven.

XCVIII.

Such was the lovely promise of its youth,
Compelled with savage ignorance to bloom:
Such would be still, had gentleness and truth
Cast o'er maturer age their rich perfume:—
Such, like the glorious orb of day, would loom
O'er wond'ring states, confêst their moral sun,—
Dispelling from the earth war's lurid gloom,
With conquest more than Cæsar ever won,—
And proving to the world millenial peace begun.

XCIX.

Ah! would that o'er the land one pulse might beat
In love to law—the lightning traverses
Its wires, the nerves of thought, with flashing feet,
Death's demon erst—an angel now to bless :—
Most distant friends exchange the swift caress,
Nor bound their converse with the mighty sea;—
Through deeper caves than ever mermaid's tress
Was looped in, mind with mind communes as free
As though time, earth, nor space had still reality.

C.

On iron bands more awful steeds are driven
Than fabled Phaeton coursed or fiery Mars;—
The mountain's granite ribs are swiftly riven
With blasts, whose ponderous shocks would break the bars
Of old Enceladus—while through the stars
Hath Science ranged—weighed, measured, analyzed—
The last, most wondrous trophy—these her wars!—
Would that such conquests were as dearly prized,
As for destruction, death, the engines she devised.

CI.

In this has modern progress distanced Eld :—
Man may progress in lore, nor bounds be set,—
And knowledge, rightly ordered, has dispelled
Dark Superstition's cloud—has burst the net
Which priestcraft spreads, its worldly gain to get :—
But in religion—ethics—what advance?
He stands the same rebellious nature yet,
Scarce changed by time and aiding circumstance,
As when from Eden turned to face earth's dread expanse.

CII.

Alas, vain man! what shall it profit thee,
To gain that world and with it lose thy soul?*
Presumptuous moth of Time!—Eternity
Stands yawning—fathomless—and this thy goal,
Whose chasing seasons swiftly o'er thee roll!—
Will science solace thee for moral death—
Typed well in him whose mad ambition stole [22]
Celestial fire, to animate the breath
Of passions doomed to die, or chain, in rocks beneath,

CIII.

The struggling Titan, with his life a prey?
That life renewed each night in worldliness,
In old transgression—which, the coming day
Must see destroyed, with aching bitterness,
Repentance,—keen remorse—the deep distress
Of conscious guilt increased with poisoned sting:—
Thus thou, whom, erst, thy God had formed to bless
All creatures—most thy kind,—to every thing,
Else the reflex of heaven, doth thy ambition bring.

CIV.

Earth is thy kingdom—there thou aim'st to reign
Successful tyrant—yet as oft the slave,
When Fortune, madly wooed, but wooed in vain,
Demands thy forfeit for the chance she gave:
Thou lowest then who sought her topmost wave,
What is thy hope, thus doomed to helpless wo,
If not that both are equal in the grave:—
That power—that strength—which keep thee down below,
That fraud and force, though here, to heaven can never go.

* Matt. xvi. 26.

4 *

CV.

The empire thou may'st rule is found within :—
Nor man nor devil can control thee there :—
Thy savage nature, snatched from natal sin,
The milk-white hues of meekness, love, may wear,
And fruits of peace to realms eternal bear:
But the wild olive must be graffed again;
Its sap, renewed, the blest luxuriance share
Of that one stock, erst planted in the plain
Of Eden—nursed in Abel—changed in murd'rous Cain.

CVI.

That tree, whose bud the starry shepherds sought,
When choirs seraphic o'er their heads resounding,
In strains of peace, good-will, the message brought,
All heathen rules of virtue, truth, confounding,—
All worldly man's high hopes of power astounding;
But, to the pure in heart,—whose eye could see *
The Husbandman—a germ, with praise redounding
To Him in Time—the looked for Plant to be,
Of love, renown, and joy, through all Eternity.

CVII.

Engrafted there—regenerate—born anew
The old corrupted nature, with its deeds,—
E'en earth would wear her Eden's earlier hue,
And angels roam again her flowery meads:
Behold, ye Mammon's slaves!—how little needs
To change her back!—on you the burden lies;—
In each the wheat and tares!—as grow their seeds
Here and hereafter shape your destinies,—
But here begin—the fruit you nurture never dies.

* Matt. v. 8.

CVIII.

Mock not your conscience, as that narrow way
You shun, to mingle in the worldly throng,—
With specious reasonings that the final day
Will find you right, when now so wholly wrong:—
The master marshals his where they belong,
Or Christ or Belial—in this lower sphere:
Few with the first—the last, his crowds among,
Makes earth the dwelling-place of lust and fear;
Affects the lamb—but runs the lion's fierce career.

CIX.

And where, oh! where his everlasting reign?
Could this existence know no mortal end,
What were it but the scene of ceaseless pain?
What Death? no king of terrors, but a friend
Sought for, in vain, the poisoned robe to rend:
To fraud and violence a constant prey,
Love could not hate—the meek dare not contend—
As now the victims of oppression's sway,
Without the cheering hope that all will pass **away.**

CX.

This life is for probation—here the mortal
Works the immortal spirit's destiny;
The embryo's growth will cease at death's dark portal,
What passes there can neither change nor die:—
Formed for the bliss of vast eternity,
God gives his wisdom and his power combined,
And ever waits his erring creature nigh,
To guide—to check—to chasten—and to wind
Toward heaven those devious steps, to pleasing sin inclined.

CXI.

If such his will, immortal man to prove,—
And fit, by tried obedience, for the sphere,
Where, with his just and true, he dwells in love,
How dare we charge him for our vileness here!
Our lusts and hate—ambition's mad career,
Which pleads religion, law, philanthropy,—
As Satan, clothed in light, would fain appear
An angel pure—to raise the battle-cry,
God! (to destroy his creatures!)—God and victory!

CXII.

Expediency—necessity—those words,
How used to perpetrate all deeds of crime:—
With them to justify, the conqueror girds
His sword for blood, and claims a cause sublime,
To track his broad red march from clime to clime:
The statesman spreads his diplomatic snare
For fraud while acting virtue's pantomime:
To both success, from human lips, will bear
Applause as likest heaven, though hell's worst hues they wear.

CXIII.

No act can be expedient if unjust;—
How well Themistocles this truth was taught![23]
None sanctioned by necessity, when trust
Is forfeited, and condemnation brought
From that one test within, so rarely sought:—
Morals are fit for nations as for men,—
And retribution is as surely wrought
For evil as reward for good—a den
Of crime for Borgia made—a paradise for Penn.

CXIV.

Man was not formed to govern—never yet
Has human wisdom, still less passion, swayed
His fellow-worms to reach that standard set
By Him whose words, professedly, are made
The ground of law, the first to be obeyed;
His teachings and our polity the same:
Example, reason, interest—all persuade,
Nay, force, through conscience, what our duties claim
From us to others—such the simple christian frame.

CXV.

Our part performed—the scrutiny begun,
By tasking self to guard our fellow's rights,
The work of government is almost done:
No more aggression, policy, invites
The demon Discord—christian love delights
To gain its victory in gaining men:
The vulgar tyrant of his kindred fights
To crush them—and they, maddened, turn again
For vengeance—making earth of murderers the den.

CXVI.

How weak, poor worm, to claim the seat of God!
Barbarians—heathen have, in former days,
Affected of their Jove the awful nod,
And snuffed the incense of unhallowed praise;
Shall we to things as base more meanly raise
Our pæans—if we stand, the truly free,
To virtue only will the thankful lays
Ascribe pre-eminence—and purity,
Joined with the needed skill, to power the passport be.

CXVII.

Our will, as creatures, must be all resigned:
Though reigning here, it cannot enter heaven;
There is but one supreme, controlling Mind—
He in the Son, to whom all power is given;—
That oneness spread to us, whose hearts have striven
To make his temple holy—such as these
Can in a nation's bulk the body leaven,
And save, like Lot, from sin's calamities;
Ah! where of late the few to change God's just decrees!

CXVIII.

Such are, in every age, the bride—the church,—
In wedlock joined, mysterious, with the Lamb:
There are no twain—and all who purely search—
The single-hearted—shall receive the palm
Promised by Him, to Israel's chief I AM*
Announced, but shown in fullness as the Son:
All nations, kindreds, tongues, who in the psalm†
Of halleluiah join, on earth begun
No more to end,—are of that church, and all are one.

CXIX.

No narrow confine bounds its mighty power:
No bond, but love to God, its chosen few
Links in a fellowship beyond the hour
Of fleeting Time, forever fresh and new:
Rebellion, hatred, discord, always grew
Without its pale—nor enters man within,
Till, born again, the soul, with heavenly hue,‡
Its life of meek obedience shall begin
To God's own light revealed—the guard and shield from sin.

* Exod. iii. 14.　　　† Rev. vii. 9.　　　‡ John iii. 5.

CXX.

Well said the stoic, greatest of his sect,*
"True piety rests in right views of God:"
The prayer from Jesus was of like effect,†
And all who, savingly, his path have trod,
Know this the entrance to the heavenly road;
Such knowledge may be termed that wicket gate,
The first in Bunyan's wondrous tale, which stood
Sole passage from the world into the strait
And narrow way—who shun it share the robber's fate.‡

CXXI.

Ah me! what snares beset the pilgrim now!
Not persecutions—not the bloody track,
Which, typed in Christian's, centuries ago
Made men familiar with the gaol—the rack—
With exile—torture—gibbet—dungeon—stake,—
Yet raised its hundred folds from martyrdom;
Foes then oppressed—now seeming friends attack,—
Bigots then fired—now Science mines the home
Of Truth—the lion raged where now the bear doth roam.

CXXII.

Th' insidious hug of friendship's false embrace
Is more disastrous than the foeman's thrust;
More dang'rous now the counterfeit, in face,
Of holy angels than the rude distrust
Which dashed her cherished emblems in the dust;
But yet, Religion, lovely and beloved,
Can yield no more to flatt'ry than to lust:
Her truth will stand to-day as much approved
As when, at Pilate's bar, in human form it moved.

* Epictetus.   † John xvii. 3.   ‡ John x. 8.

CXXIII.

None dare deny that perfectness divine:
The age for ribald scoff has passed away;—
A decent fear—a proud respect—confine
All vulgar outrage from the light of day:—
Voltaire's coarse sneer, and Paine's malignant bray,
Have lost their echoes in oblivion's gloom:—
That life, that godlike life, has cast its ray,
Though Envy quenched the source, beyond her tomb,
Confessed the moral Sun whose beams all Time illume.

CXXIV.

Yet, though the lion's grip may scarcely tear,—
The poisoned fang, the kick, no danger bring,
Nor rough caress while hugs the slavering bear,
She dreads the treachery of the panther's spring:
Dreads the smooth friend—whose soft imagining
Is clothed in all the iris hues of heaven—
Whose silken praises o'er her virtues fling
A robe, to which more fatal power is given
Than that Alcmena's son in death had vainly riven.

CXXV.

How sweetened now, for all, the deadly draught!—
How gilded o'er the surely poisoned pill!
Like gods their nectar, men have freely quaffed
The fascinating cup, nor dreamed of ill:
New gospels—shorn of vulgar miracle—
New lives of Him, that wondrous man of men,
The claims which Science sternly makes, fulfil,
Bedecked with splendors that the polished pen
Of fancy, genius, strews to dazzle mortal ken.

CXXVI.

How pure his lovely youth from touch of sin,
As, rapt with ancient seers in Hebrew lore,
And, self-deceived, he felt the throes begin,
Whose longings—pains—the sought Messiah bore—
Scarce conscious of the dangerous crown he wore,
'Till claimed for proof of superhuman sway:
Then, forced to ill by circumstance, he tore
The snowy robe of innocence away,
Became imposture's tool, and shunned the blaze of day.

CXXVII.

Such is the outline—stripped of honied phrase,[24]—
Perchance the best—that skeptic Science draws:—
What marvel, when the corner-stone she lays,
Rests on the quicksands of material laws!
She sees, for all effects, no other cause
Than what poor Reason traces with the sense:
Wrapped in themselves, their mutual applause,
These pagods of the mind, with vain pretence
Of knowledge—know not man, much less Omnipotence.

CXXVIII.

Yet blame them not—they act but as their kind,—
And aim to level Superstition's shrine,—
Whose dogmas dark its fetters strongly bind
O'er shackled souls, in schemes miscalled divine:
If human learning theories assign
For God,—inscrutable unless revealed,—
Our censure, when too sweeping, may malign
These sometimes rude iconoclasts, who wield
Their weapons in attack on Truth's polemic field.

5   D

CXXIX.

Something of good we draw from every source,—
As poisons serve for healing, used with skill:—
Fires—pestilence—and war, with furious force,
Have swept from lands full many a cause of ill,
And monstrous growths oft great designs fulfil:
The potsherd, 'gainst the potsherd's broken ring,
Will save the perfect vase that does not spill;—
And Logic's ponderous blows to truth may bring
New searchings for that fount, whence only it can spring.

CXXX.

Nought but the false is shaken—heaven and earth *
Of human scheming—that, alone, remains
Which owes existence to the promised birth,†
Typed by that wondrous life on Judah's plains—
Whose name,—whose power,—increasing, ever reigns:
The vulture's eye,—our keen philosophy—
Hath seen it not:—her lofty walk disdains ‡
A path so hid—no lion hath passed by
The Lamb's low, narrow track of meek humility.

CXXXI.

All sense, all reason—fail to comprehend
The things of God,—the merely natural man,
In science trained, his measured step may wend
With sure advance through nature's mazy plan:
The stars may weigh—their distant courses span—
Or, turning back on past eternity,
Prove how our earth her myriad ages ran,—
Produce her rock-bound dates that cannot lie,
To shake our cherished faith in ancient prophecy.

* Heb. xii. 27.　　　† Isaiah ix. 6.　　　‡ Job xxviii. 7.

CXXXII.

What then! if much of lore that stands in doubt
Beyond our grasp—as local Eden's tale
Of man, created pure—by sin cast out—
And swiftly waving sword to guard its pale,
Shall, or in fact, or metaphor prevail,
Or nearest truth, of both composed we deem:
Can such discrepancies *in terms* assail
The misty sources of that fertile stream,—
Our spirit's Nile, whose flood is there th' inspiring theme.

CXXXIII.

As well attempt to show the blind from birth
The gorgeous colors of the evening cloud,
When sunset splendors, fading o'er the earth,
Heaven's vault with richest hues of Iris crowd,—
As saving Faith to him, who ne'er has bowed
His stubborn nature to Christ's gentle yoke;—
To those, alone, with inward sense endowed,
His clear, revealing language ever spoke,
And speaks, with surer speech than wisest man or book.

CXXXIV.

Men are the witnesses—and, as they hear,
They testify of knowledge—they have seen
With more than mortal sight, and sense more clear
Than carnal eye or ear hath ever been,
That promised life bathed in eternal sheen;—
And, pilgrims wandering through a world of wo,
Despised and mocked while scorning joys terrene,
Their works, their self-denial, sufferings, show
That hearts sincere have yearned to lighten sin below.

CXXXV.

The records tell of these—their thoughts, their deeds,—
The purposed wonders of that Power divine
Which ruled and wrought within them—he who reads
With quickened soul, with spirit bowed, like mine,
As in a glass will see his glories shine,—
His cloak for sin with stubborn nature cast,*
When heart was stony—hands incarnadine :—
In theirs he views his own experience past;
Their holy triumph proves that his will come at last.

CXXXVI.

Talk not of outward miracles—the sight
Of all that Jesus wrought in Galilee,
When clothed with fullness of eternal might,
Could scarce increase their firm belief in me :
Had I been present when he walked its sea,
Had I beheld the maniac drop his chain,
Restored, and meekly bending at the knee,
Which, as a child, he ne'er would leave again,—
Though sense might give me strength, the proof would press
        in vain.

CXXXVII.

Or more, a witness at that humble grave,
To hear the language, "Lazarus, come forth,"
My soul no greater evidence would have
Of Him than when He quickened me from earth,
As dead—to higher life—His second birth ;—
When Light above the brightness of the sun,
Illumed, to blind ;—but never outward hearth
Received such glorious ray, near ev'ning dun,
When richest tints proclaim day's lengthened journey run.

* John xv. 22.

CXXXVIII.

I too have passed the skeptic's gloomy phase :
Beheld all nature bound in changeless laws ;—
Proved that, in endless cycles, she displays
No will, no being—'twas effect from cause ;
That cause, again effect, its movement draws
Once known, alike, eternally the same :
None keener to detect the seeming flaws,
Which make e'en sacred writ the standing game
For fledgelings partly taught—for critics but in name.

CXXXIX.

In manhood's strength, with all that might rejoice
Ambition, love, content, and honest pride,—
As Abram when he heard and knew the voice,
Commanding change which Reason would deride,—
So I, and speechless struck, obeyed my Guide ;—
Nor asked of human counsel strength nor aid,—
My course too clear to be with doubt allied,—
My seeming as a fool to worldlings made,—
But yet to shrink were crime like his who Christ betrayed.

CXL.

And, giving all for all—surrend'ring life,
First nature's yearning for terrestrial things,
To cast on Him the burden of that strife
Which every added tie to prudence brings,
I've known the depth of human sufferings :
Yet known, again, His gracious promise true,   .
The hundred fold returned on angels' wings :
Have seen, as Job, e'en outward earth anew
Give back her richest fruits—more rich with heavenly dew.

5 *

CXLI.

How oft, in turning to that priceless page
Of God's like dealings with his saints of yore,
Its truthful records would the pangs assuage
Of many an ill that nature hardly bore—
Of prickly paths which pilgrims trod before:—
But most with him—whose form, whose sacred head,
The crown of thorns and seamless garment wore:
What life were ours had he not freely bled,
What hope for us, were he not raised again when dead?

CXLII.

Behold, ye skeptics! here your final goal!
If God may never Nature contravene,
The body dies—but where th' immortal soul,
Forever past from this material scene!
Faith fails you—and the things which have not been,
In your philosophy can never be,—
Your Science has no staff on which to lean
In groping through that dark futurity,
But all is doubt—despair;—death closes hopelessly.

CXLIII.

Yet, had ye reasoned from his brother sleep,
Beheld all sense so locked, and so profound,
As 'twere annihilation—scarce less deep
Than when corruption's taint hath floated round,
You might have deemed it miracle to bound
Back, with the radiant morn, to joyous life;
Your sleep was death—nor sight, nor touch, nor sound,
Nor dreamy thought, gave evidence of strife
In this material frame, where all with change is rife.

CXLIV.

This wondrous microcosm defies your skill!—
No knife nor chemic test can aid you there:—
The blood with life its every gland may fill,
And each have different functions—tell me where
The cause these cells such diverse products bear!
You scan, observe, and call it nature's law,
Known when results with like results compare:—
With that conclusion comes your fatal flaw—
Your facts are noted—there you leave them and withdraw.

CXLV.

Show me the soul!—the all controlling will,
To guard, to guide this tenement of clay!
That stubborn source of every human ill,
Untamed—of good, if meekly it obey:
Deprived of every sense but touch, its ray
Will reach in converse from that inner shrine:[25]
And there the immortal being holds its sway,
As perfect, pure, as gold within the mine—
Concealed, but none the less that creature stamped divine.

CXLVI.

What finite there in nature infinite
Controls—upholds—the one eternal Mind—
Whose laws alike all ages, creatures fit,
In matter changeless as in living kind:
But man responsible, whom morals bind,
Like Him with balanced will, unfettered, free,
Hath heaven's high hope to sin perverse consigned,
Wrecked innocence o'er dark rebellion's sea,
Where shoreless waves roll on in ceaseless misery.

CXLVII.

Those laws may change for changing moods of men:
Heaven's highest, constant purpose is to save
The self-willed tenants of earth's savage den,
From hell e'en here—but most beyond the grave:
God aims that every soul the means shall have
To pass, with will subdued, the gates of bliss:
Forever theirs the guilt who madly brave
That life to come—precursors warn in this,
As War—yet small the taste of endless wretchedness.

CXLVIII.

But vain my task to reason with the blind!
And none so blind as they who will not see,—
Whose conscience, feelings, soul, those fetters bind
Of pride in human science:—sophistry
With them finds idols under every tree:
What were my power when, where the Godhead dwelt
In fullness, nought but love, humility,
The contrite heart his gracious presence felt—
Rejected from that fane where worldly wisdom knelt.

CXLIX.

No power can reach *that* wisdom from beneath—
Whose chiefest aids, ambition, envy, pride,
Draw, like the eastern king, from human breath
The incense of the lip—they, erst, denied
In Eden God's behest—turned Eve aside,
And all her myriad race, from innocence,
And now, their half oped portals casting wide,
With claims to light, with learning's vast pretence,
They fain would prostrate all we love and reverence.

CL.

Alas! how much may lie within the power
Of man, destroying what a host has built!
Th' Ephesian pride one torch—one transient hour
Effaced—to blazon but the name of guilt:
A world-wide fame like Penn's has found a jilt,
No Muse, in hist'ry's brilliant half romance:[26]
Th' assassin's knife hath, in a moment, spilt
The hopes of millions—witness him of France,
Though nearer home such thought may turn our mournful
  glance.

CLI.

The poison goes broadcast—the antidote,
However sure, can only reach the few,—
And vain our aims to follow seeds that float
Widely and subtle as malarious dew:
And what the soil! no fungi ever grew
With half the rank luxuriance of this.
Shall fancy, eloquence, conceal from view,
With robes of heaven—with all that gorgeous dress
Can lend, the human soul's most loathsome nakedness!

CLII.

Man mortal! God but myth! an empty name!
And science—matter—nature deified!
Christ, gifted more than most, as others came,
As others lived, and loved, and taught, and died!
This the new gospel! all beyond denied!
All faith—all hope in future scenes to live!
Such the dark tribute Folly pays to Pride,—
Such all that earthly man to men can give—
And all the unregen'rate heart may yet receive.

CLIII.

What can you substitute who aim to shake
The strong foundation of the christian's faith?
What staff, in lieu of grounded hopes that break
The force of earthly ills, the shock of death?
The upas venom of your numbing breath
The valley's sod with driest bones will strew,*
But nought of life be present till He saith,
As through the seer, that heavenly winds may blow,
And from chaotic drought a living army grow.

CLIV.

That cloud of witnesses will rise again;
It hath, in every clime—in every age—
Despite the scourge of Superstition's reign,
And dark malevolence of priestly rage:
The same, with added power, can take the gage
Of battle, cast on learning's slippery field:
The craven counterfeits are they who wage
This warfare of the Lamb, and, forced to yield,
Prove but their armor weak, which Truth has never steeled.

CLV.

Such combat here resembles that in heaven,
When Michael fought the dragon and his crew—
Or that, perchance, had man in Eden striven
To keep the great commandment, just and true,
Eat not, or die, of self-willed pride, which grew
Rebellion—knowledge vain to be as gods:
Weak, fallen man, too late his weakness knew;—
How strong. of innocence. the blest abodes;
How dark those devious paths his wretched offspring plods.

* Ezekiel xxxvii. 1–10.

CLVI.

But what the stake? the myriads yet to be!
Souls—but as seeds which never fructify,
Or, claiming joys that immortality
Shall cherish, in the hopes of those who die,
To live with all th' angelic host on high:
They needs must grow—if bent or stunted twig,
Parched with the drought of man's philosophy,—
For nought the zealous husbandman may dig;
The cursed—the withered tree ne'er bore the fruitful fig.

CLVII.

God works by means—e'en nature proves it true,
In all the vast profusion of her store;—
Her countless germs, with neither rain nor dew,
Pass into dust, as lifeless as before:
The mind itself would vainly seek to soar
Cramped—crippled in primeval ignorance;—
So with the moral frame—the man—who wore [27]
Mind—matter, as a garment—his advance
Owes much to early care—to genial circumstance.

CLVIII.

As in the sire the offspring feels the sin,
Some taint—some consequence through Time descend,
Else had all equal—pure—and perfect been,
Created thus—so may our teachings lend,
For ages, strength to what we now defend:
And blest are they who, in the Truth, proclaim
God Sovereign Lord—and mortals comprehend:
Such the white stone are promised, and new name,
In light fore'er to shine as shines the starry frame.

CLIX.

These form the church—the militant, on earth—
Too oft the mark for sneer—for bitterest scorn;—
The Pharisee still vaunts his deeds of worth—
His alms, of pride—his acts, of hatred born:
The Sadducee, as erst, would still adorn
This life with joys derived, to end with sense,
Nor reckoning kept for resurrection's morn,
His wealth—his love for fame—his proud pretence
To knowledge,—prove his master's kingdom *is* from hence.

CLX.

Yet vain his hopes of pleasure in the grasp:—
They vanish—yours, the daily cross who bear,
Are treasured in a more than earthly clasp:—
And loving angels watch, with heavenly care,
That badge of sorrow or of shame you wear;
Theirs and your Master ever knows his own:
A few more trials here will fill your share
Of suff'rings left behind—that victory won,
You stand in robes of white forever round his throne.

CLXI.

'Tis there the church triumphant, with the palm,
Emblem of conquest o'er all powers below,—
Will see its former head, the mystic Lamb,
The Judge of all—the source from whence shall flow
Those streams of love which it alone can know:—
Then conflicts, sorrows, pains, will pass away,
And hunger, thirst, and night depart, and wo,
From scenes of nought but bliss with perfect day,—
From realms where God will rule with everlasting sway.

CLXII.

But weak the thought to find His rule below—
This world is Cæsar's—Christ is crucified :
Could earth's proud symbol grace that heavenly brow,
Messiah, crowned, had never bled and died*
As then, from Envy's schemes and human pride :
A nation here his kingdom might have known,
Had Justice, Mercy, Truth, remained allied,
As first they sat upon their triple throne,
Like India's three-fold god—but joined and fused in one.

CLXIII.

Nor, failing thus, can ever man again
Hail morn so bright—as none was seen before,
Since when, created pure, God's perfect reign
Through him, obedient, blossomed Eden o'er
With every fruit but that rebellion bore ;—
Yet here, where man, redeemed, regained that sway,
And proved its rule on earth's most savage shore,
'Twas glorious dawn of direful, lurid day—
And Hope, Aurora's star, hath long since passed away.

CLXIV.

Salvation is a work in every heart ;—
The reign millenial must in each begin :—
Perfected grown, its christian fruits impart
The power, through him, to others bound in sin,
And thus new converts from its courses win ;—
As the pure leaven spreads, the old and new
Are joined in that where nature hath not kin,
Mysterious wedlock of the just and true,
The church with Him, her spouse, the endless ages through.

* John xv. 18-20.

6

CLXV.

Then weaned from meaner aims to place above
Our eye in singleness, with steadfast gaze,
Each added pace the soul may make will prove
Blest harbinger of love and lengthened days:
Example preaches more than loudest praise:
The end approaching brighter grows the crown,
More sure the peace that flows in wisdom's ways:
The light we bear within us, not alone
For us will shine—its beams on all around are thrown.

CLXVI.

That light the life—the only life of men,*
If e'er redeemed to reach a heavenly sphere:
The nations saw its beauty break through Penn
And kindred spirits, dwelling ever near
The Source of truth—of virtue's high career:
The good old gospel, then anew revealed,
The same to-day, and yesterday—fore'er,—
The one eternal law, still unrepealed—
Brings peace to every heart, which grace of God hath sealed.

CLXVII.

And He, all love, ne'er broke the bruisèd reed,
Nor quenched the smoking flax, till victory
Raised in the earthly heart his lowly seed,
Oppressed with worldly-mindedness, to be
A plant of high renown—the heavenly tree:
Such fruit 'twill bear again as then it bore,
Thrice blest to all around on earth—if we
Yield, passive, as they erst who trod our shore:—
That Power will work in us which wrought in them before.

* John i. 4.

CLXVIII.

Thus for Eternity preparing—man
Becomes the light—is made the guide in Time—
Fulfils his mission in redemption's plan,
His own secured—atones his brother's crime
By labors meek, or sacrifice sublime:
Such for a fallen world the sinless one,—
And such, for those around, in every clime,
The race which true obedience hath run:
We by adoption claim—but he the only son.

CLXIX.

Pre-eminence is his—and his all power
In heaven and earth :—who would with him partake,
Must drink his cup—must know night's darkest hour,
When kindred, friends, and followers forsake,
Forerunner of a darker day to break:
That day, eclipsed, must witness nature die,
Ere from its sepulchre the life awake,
Which bears the soul, redeemed, to dwell on high:
The cross precedes the crown—bliss springs from Calvary.

CLXX.

Whate'er the cost, his words, his sinless life,
Our law supreme should be, our cherished guide :—
Howe'er the reckless world may dwell in strife,
The christian knows no war but that with pride,
Ambition, lust, and ills to these allied :—
When their dominion in his soul shall cease,
The heavenly hosts are ever on his side—
With him, co-workers for the sure increase
Of their great Master's sway—th' eternal Prince of Peace.

ELEGY

ON THE LOSS OF A SISTER.

DEATH! of all teachers, thou alone art heard,
   With vast Eternity's tremendous theme:
Thy awful sermon needs no sounding word,
   Thy spectral voice no oratoric gleam.

From the cold corse, where laughing life so late
   Shone forth, luxuriantly, 'mid joy and love,
Thou speak'st, in thunder, the decree of fate,
   And point'st, with startling truth, to God above.

Thou preachest sure, great monitor of man,
   And piercest keenly to the stubborn heart;
What lips so eloquent as those I scan,
   Now closed forever by thy marble dart!

What eye of fire as quickly thrills the soul,
   As the pale calmness of that icy brow!
So lately moving with the mind's control,
   Whose vanished light illumes no longer now.

64

Th' unearthly rapture of that tranquil face,
  The lingering semblance of the seraph fled,
Must yield, ere long, its heaven-reflected grace
  To the dark mantle of the mould'ring dead.

The form and features, to whose varied play,
  Health, youth, and beauty all their magic gave,
Will soon be shrouded in their kindred clay,
  And dust with dust commingled in the grave.

Affection's tearful eye may look its last
  On thee, the sad remains of youth and love,—
And, turning o'er the record of the past,
  The soul be girt to join thee yet above.

Not all in vain thy prematurèd doom,
  If, by this awful dispensation taught,
We vow repentance at thy lowly tomb,
  And seek that grace thy spirit daily sought.

Lo! as I linger o'er thy lifeless form,
  And weep thy transit to the realms of bliss,
Dost thou not gaze with pity on the worm,
  Whose groveling nature shuns thy world for this?

Dost thou not, spirit, freed from grosser clay,
  Look down with wonder on our mean desires,
That reach the paltriest passions of a day,
  And pant but coldly for celestial fires?

Oh! in the dust all lowly as I wind,
  A reptile seeker for the dross of earth,
Gazing on thee, this once unsullied mind
  Revives its traces of a heavenly birth.

6 *   E

Taught by thy awful eloquence, I turn
  To feed my spirit on immortal food;
And, in the mighty loss which now we mourn,
  Perceive the warning finger of my God.

A year, a day, an hour, may number me
  Among the victims of the spoiler, Death;
Proud as I am, could I be ranked with thee,
  Or, firm in faith, resign my parting breath?

Alas! that treasure, priceless to the soul,
  But little love, less heed hath had from mine:
With spurning heel I've burst the meek control,
  Enjoined o'er passion's sway by lips divine.

Unfettered, wild, and lawless have I roamed,
  An aimless wanderer o'er life's doubtful sea;
Eager to ride where most the breakers foamed,—
  Of Time as reckless as Eternity.

With other fools I've knelt at glory's shrine,
  And worshipped wildly proud ambition's god;
Yet now, in turning humbly unto thine,
  Could kiss, with thankful joy, th' avenging rod.

Mysterious presence! from thy voiceless tongue,
  I hear the truth proclaimed by all that die—
Heard when thus lonely or amid the throng;
  "Time is—Time was—Time's past—Death hovers nigh."

Death! the great harbinger of all beyond
  That unknown region, dread, unfathomed sea;—
Where mortal foot hath never entrance found,
  Whose only passage, naked, lies through thee.

From thee, thou mould'ring corse, this lesson learned,
  Haste then, my soul, to seek that lowly way,
Whose narrow, rugged path hath ever turned
  The weary pilgrim to eternal day.

With humble hope I'll 'bide that hour of rest,
  Each thought to God, and holiest purpose given,
When Death shall summon me to join the blest,
  And meet thy spirit in its native heaven.

LINES

WRITTEN IN AN ALBUM.

THERE are friendships here which bind us,
  Ere the tongue of time hath told
Days, nay, hours can often wind us
  In a love that ne'er is cold.

There are souls prepared in heaven,
  Which as magnets meet on earth,
And the chain eterne is riven,
  Linked by ties of kindred worth.

There are hearts, though reft asunder,
  Malice has no power to part;
Though the world may gaze with wonder,
  Friendship rules their every start.

There are spirits, though in pleasure,
  Fate has fanned the springing flame,
Still, when sorrows fill their measure,
  They can love, and love the same.

Aye, and minds on soaring pinions
  Grasping at the glorious wreath—
Though they scorn earth's puppet minions,
  Yet can follow—e'en to death.

There are souls to all around them
  Haughty—dark—and full of wo,
But when kindred spirits sound them,
  Then, oh! then their bosoms glow.

These are they, to all else lonely,
  Who in silence shun the crowd—
With their thoughts communing only—
  From the vulgar and the proud.

Such I deem thy lofty spirit,
  Formed above the mould of art,—
Such I deem thy social merit,
  Such, oh! such I deem thy heart.

A PORTRAIT.

WHEN ancient art would, in its dreams of heaven,
    Essay to mould a fitting type of love,
To human forms its ceaseless care was given,
    And sculpture mirrored man his hopes above:
But through long years its patient toil had striven
    From fixed enduring stone the soul to move,
Ere, in the bending statue, woman stood
The Greek ideal of the pure and good.

Through later times, inspired by papal Rome,
    Her charms have tasked the painter's magic skill,—
And all that wealth or power in Christendom
    Could yield, to fire the soul, was his at will:
From Guido's touch her varied graces come,—
    From Raphael's master-hand her beauties fill
The kneeling suppliant with his hopes of bliss,
In brighter worlds beyond the ken of this.

But oh! all perfect as her sculptured form,
    Of more than mortal loveliness, may be,
All rich her features, limned in tints, as warm
    As sunset splendors o'er the summer's sea,—

70

All potent as their influence to charm
 A ravished world of worshippers—to me
Both concentrated stores of art and grace
Must yield in beauty to that living face.

Mine is the taste which seeks not from the stone,
 Nor yet the canvas, so divinely wrought,—
That true ideal which has e'er outshone
 The highest graces yet by genius caught;—
My dreams of such perfection take their tone
 From feelings far beyond all earthly thought;—
Nor sculptor's skill, nor painter's power, can teach
The truth that sensual man would vainly reach.

Far as the faith I hold transcends the show
 Which priestly craft has schemed to sway the heart;
Far as it towers above all types below,
 That pagan systems claimed from wondrous art,—
So sits serenely on that placid brow,
 A pure ideal of the better part;—
The perfect glory of man's second birth,—
The blest reality of heaven on earth.

In meekness, patience, and unbounded love,
 In calm submission to the daily cross,—
In humble waiting for its Guide above;—
 In holding wealth, fame, honors, all as dross,
To reach what man contemns, but saints approve,
 That peace, unknown since blissful Eden's loss,
Thine is the faith whose living power alone
Can bring the wanderer up to Mercy's throne.

And dream I wildly in beholding there
 The pure embodiment of love and hope;

Of sweet contentment 'neath those tresses fair,
 Where meekness, mind, and loftiest feelings cope,
And blend divinely from that lustrous pair
 Of eyes more deeply blue than, through the scope
Of ether, peers round Cynthia's orb serene,
When o'er the night she reigns unclouded queen.

Judge I not truly, as by instinct driven,
 I see combined all human loveliness
With Faith and Peace, those attributes of heaven,
 That there the seraph sits in mortal dress;—
That there its perfect type to earth is given,
 Where centres all of both that lives to bless:—
If so, your beaming face and plain attire
May well command the homage of my lyre.

THE TRIUMPH OF PATIENCE.

"Have pity upon me, have pity upon me, O ye my friends: for the hand of God hath touched me.

"Why do ye persecute me as God, and are not satisfied with my flesh?

"Oh that my words were now written! oh that they were printed in a book!

"That they were graven with an iron pen and lead in the rock for ever!

"For I know that my Redeemer liveth, and that he shall stand at the latter day upon the earth:

"And though, after my skin, worms destroy this body, yet in my flesh shall I see God:

"Whom I shall see for myself, and mine eyes shall behold, and not another; though my reins be consumed within me."

JOB XIX. 21-27.

LOW sinks that form, before whose high command
Princes erst stood, from many a distant land;
Whose stately presence and majestic mien,
In solemn grandeur, graced each public scene,
Whose day's meridian shone with matchless ray,
When all was his—wealth, friends, and regal sway.

Low sinks he now, as blow, succeeding blow,
Has dashed to atoms every joy below,—
Has stripped his home, destroyed his outward wealth,
Nor left him children's love nor kindlier health;—

7

Alone, in ashes, bruised from heel to head,
He sits entreating death, and worse than dead.

Yet are his crowded sorrows least from these,
While treachery tempts him to a sinful ease,
While she, to whom his earlier love was given,
Would, for relief, renounce his hope in heaven;—
While friends around, to superhuman woes
Add pangs of torture more than direst foes,
With cold hypocrisy defame his worth,
And aim to snatch his dearest gem on earth.

Worn to the last that patience-lengthened chain,
Exhausted Nature feels her struggles vain;
Reason's high hope and Wisdom's treasured lore
Succumb beneath their complicated war,
Till, bowed with agony of mind and frame,
He begs their pity—wrecked in all but fame.

Shall he, whose fast integrity remains
Untarnished thus through more than mortal pains—
Shall he—deserted—helpless—sink to death?
No! in the moment of that passing breath,
Which claimed compassion, upward sprang his soul
Beyond the reach of earth, and hell's control,—
Power, life, and light were, in an instant, given,
And thus he spake, as one inspired of heaven.

      Oh! that my voice,
The echo of that living glory round me,
With words of Him, whose quickening love hath found me,
      Might bid the world rejoice;—
That the great truth, whose sound my lips shall sever,
Were deeply graven in the rock forever.

I know, I know,
That my Redeemer lives, and his appearing
Shall, in the hearts of those his judgments fearing,
        Stand over all below;—
His feet shall trample that which is of earth,
And guide the spirit through its heavenly birth.

        Though to the worms
This broken carcass and its frame be given,
Yet, even here, the sight of Him in heaven,
        Amid the mingled storms
Which beat my bark, shall smooth its devious way,
Till moored forever in the realms of day.

The proof is o'er, the testing trial passed,
And suffering patience wins its crown at last,
He, who hath humbled lowly in the dust,
Repays, an hundred-fold, unfalt'ring trust;—
Though through a transient hour of darkness tost,
While Faith remained, the ship could ne'er be lost;—
Though in the hindmost part, forgot in sleep,
The Master watches o'er the angry deep,
Moves in the roar of elemental strife,
And wakes, to bring Omnipotence to life.

MATTER AND SPIRIT.

A FEW short hours, and thou wert there,
   Communing, soul with soul:
But now no sense can fathom where
   Thy spirit holds control.

The form remains; that glazèd eye,
   Now lustreless in death,—
Those pallid lips, so tranquilly,
   We seem to feel their breath.

I watched thee as the ebbing life
   Sunk, sense by sense, away—
I knew *thee* till the closing strife—
   But now there lies the *clay*.

Where art thou? all I ever saw,
   Before me still remains—
I miss but that controlling law
   When life o'er matter reigns.

Could I, with Science' mimic art,
  Reanimate thy form?
Behold *thee* when each quivering start,
  Convulsive, moves that arm?

Ah! no; too surely thou hast left
  The home, so lately thine:—
The tenement lies there, bereft—
  To us a worthless shrine.

Thou, the in-dwelling soul—to me
  But yesterday so near,
Art shrouded now in mystery
  Beyond communion here.

I may not doubt that perfect all,
  Thou livest yet—though there,
Beneath that dread funereal pall,
  Each atom, thine, they bear.

If thus with thee, thou spirit friend,
  Now bosomed in thy God,
Vainly I seek to comprehend
  What dwelt in that abode,—

How shall I dare, with impious thought,
  To image Him in space,
Whose power omnipotent hath wrought,
  And works in every place.

How, foolishly, essay to rear
  The tower, of human skill,
Whose top shall reach th' eternal sphere
  Where hymning seraphs dwell!

Cease, then, my speculative lore
  To pierce the realms of death;—
All that I may is to adore
  In deep, unfaltering faith.

Thou art, and God is; and beyond
  No clue to man is given:
That truth can bridge the vast profound,
  Connecting earth with heaven.

ELIZABETH FRY.

TIME moves in cycles, not revolving years,
  Whose rolling course the same dull impress bears;
From age to age he plods his lengthened way,
O'er empires born to flourish and decay.
These on the historic page alike disclose
The tale, in fraud and war, of human woes.
Too rare, indeed, across its desert path
One virtuous act redeems an age of wrath;
More rarely still a clustering group appears
Of those who rather dry than cause its tears.

Should some intent and curious student pore
Through all our ancient oracles of lore,
Scan, work by work, the records of the past,
To what conclusion must he come at last?
What, but that man is more a beast of prey
Than formed or fit for Virtue's heavenly sway?
That term, to us a synonym of love,
The savage eagle types, but not the dove.

To Roman ears brute valor bore the name;
To Spartan, theft was glory, fraud was fame;
Athena's justice, vaunted to the sky,
Was *but* to shun the vilest treachery;[28]
Ascend from earth above, their gods are given
Stained o'er with deeds far worthier hell than heaven;
The childish phantoms of a madman's brain,
A monstrous brood of Superstition's reign.

The classic stream, from earth's primeval morn,
Her thousand heroes to our age has borne;
But ah! how few exemplars worth the name,
Of all its throng that swell the tide of fame!
How sparse the meek, the lowly, and the good,
How poorly noticed o'er its rolling flood!
Pride, pomp, and power, and savage fierceness bear
The loftiest praise of human genius there,
The historic pen, the poet's strain inspire
To gild their rayless peaks with sacred fire,
While christian virtue, in its meek career,
Receives a tribute from the passing sneer;
Too much a stranger, like its sons, on earth,
For groveling man to recognize its worth.

Yet, though so oft the desecrated muse
Her loftiest strains to noblest themes refuse,
And pass neglected humble goodness o'er
To crown her heroes drenched in human gore,
A lowly harp would fain essay to sing
On subjects worthy of a Homer's string.
Too lately gone from harvest-fields below
Are they its feeble notes would herald now:
All fresh the labors of their glorious day,
Whose closing twilight scarce has passed away:

Their too familiar forms forbid the praise
Which distant stranger-tongues would loudly raise;
Their works, so recent wrought, too dazzling yet,
Those uncut jewels Time alone can set.

But though so nearly known and fondly loved,
So lately heard and seen, and scarcely moved,
All warm and lifelike, from thine active sphere,
No years, Eliza, needs thy high career.
From Newgate's cell to distant Sydney cove,
Thy name is synonym of truth and love.
As from the dark and frozen pole is given
That wondrous light to arch the face of heaven,
Serene and brilliant o'er the Arctic snows,
Its modest radiance blushing as it glows;
So from that rock-ribbed den of vice and crime
A moral light has flashed to every clime.
The gentle, roseate rays of human love
Once more reflected from their Source above,
Such as have shone through all that glorious band,
Who, like their Master, moved at Truth's command.
Thine was the triumph of the conqueror's car,
Not in the horrid clash of outward war;
Not on the mangled limbs of hostile foes,
But over Vice, and all her train of woes.
Thine was the glorious lot to show that Faith,
Whose quickening power is stronger far than Death,
In wondrous beauty to a gazing world,
From depths whence every kindred sway was hurled.
Of the long line of Truth's meek pioneers,
Through want, oppression, wretchedness, and tears,
Through hatred, darkest cruelty, and blood,
Outcasts and aliens to the bad and good,

Thine was the happier task, with equal zeal,
To storm unwilling hearts in Love's appeal;
To force, in proofs, resistless Virtue's claim,
And float triumphant to a world-wide fame.

Yet not to thee alone these strains belong,
Though first and foremost in my humble song;
Thou art but one of that close-kindred band,
Whose gentle light illumes each christian land.
Around thee cluster, in thy radiant sphere,
Souls scarcely less to Mercy's mission dear;
A brother's* love and labors strengthened thine,
And with thy wreath his laurels well entwine:
With thee, with him shall pensive Memory dwell,
And mourning hearts in thankful rapture swell,
As, kindling high the flame which Virtue rears,
Such love, such works as yours shall melt to tears;
Time will but hallow names so nearly joined
In worthiest triumphs of immortal mind,
As undivided as in yonder sphere
Ye live more radiant and forever dear.
Nor at your festive board in proud array,
When nearest kindred met to mark the day,
Were you the only oracles of Fame,
The Rolands of your far-ennobled name:
Another there, with tall, commanding mien,†
As fitly graced the glories of the scene;
He on whose lips the British Senate hung,
While Genius, Pathos, Mercy, moved his tongue;
When thoughts and words, as burning as her clime,
Made Afric's countless wrongs a cause sublime.

* Joseph John Gurney.
† Thomas Fowell Buxton, her brother-in-law.

Yet onward still, my muse : another there,*
For whom e'en now we shed th' unbidden tear;
A meek-eyed elder plodding in your train,
To die in harness o'er the distant main.
Another still, and others might succeed,
To nations known in many a glorious deed;
Some, like yourselves, beyond the ills of Time,
And some yet wanderers through this lower clime.
But to the worthy dead alone I raise
The passing tribute of my feeble praise;
The living, loved, and honored, claim from me
No herald's meed to dim futurity.

Say, where, in all the chronicles of yore,
A brighter group has kindred virtue bore?
What, to the sterling worth of one like this,
Rome's lofty claim for Fabian nobleness?
Her vaunted family of warriors bled
With kindred butchers on their heaps of dead;
Their proud ambition bounded by their name
To fight and win the patriot's doubtful fame.
What fair Cornelia's jewels, dimmed in blood
By passion fierce and dire intestine feud?
Or, aptly matched in Alba's earlier day,
Her three with Rome's in wild, fraternal fray,
When armies stood spectators of the fight,
And brutal murder crowned the victor's right!
Shall such, the savage bull-dog's praise, be ours,
Who claim companionship with heavenly powers;
Whom God designed with angel hosts to stand
Before His throne, one ever-mingling band?
Forbid the thought in every honest breast,
Whose faltering tongue has christian faith professed;

* William Forster.

Forbid the praise to men, whose highest skill
Is but the warrior's pride, the most to kill.
A nobler aim our gospel message bears,
To heal their wounded hearts, to dry their tears;
To seek the haunts of wretchedness and wo,
And point whence perfect peace alone can flow.
Yet oh! of all the wars which man may wage,
No nobler contest can his powers engage
Than that with Self, the demon bound within,
Whose rule is service to a world of sin.
Without this conquest, vain the victor's wreath;
With it he triumphs over more than Death;
The transient trophies of his earthly sway
Will pass, as valueless, with years away;
But in that birth where stubborn nature dies,
He starts, a champion for the heavenly prize;
Reaps even here the hundred-fold of gain,
And bears his blessings to an endless reign.

Thus, as the muse your harvest-field surveys,
She yields the tribute of unmingled praise;
For such exemplars to a sinful earth
But justly claims the crown of christian worth—
That loftiest fame for pure, unselfish love,
In wisdom leading man to bliss above.
Long may we seek a group like yours in vain,
Through rolling years on earth's ensanguined plain—
Long, long, Eliza, wait for one like thee again.

ON A SHIP FOUNDERING AT SEA.

NOT in the field,
    Where squadrons charging o'er the dead and dying,
And the gashed victim in his blood is lying,
    Life's last-drawn sigh to yield,
Does Death, the grisly king, his terrors bear,
Robed in the gloomiest mantle of despair.

        The stirring sounds
Of war's tremendous game above him ringing;
The awful thunders o'er his senses, winging
    To thousands more the wounds
Which laid him low, are antidotes to pain,
And smooth his passage to oblivion's reign.

        Nor on the couch,
When, through protracted pangs, his pallid fingers
Part, one by one, each fainter hope that lingers,
    Brings the fell monarch's touch
Its keenest throb, its agonizing throe,
To free the sufferer from a world of wo.

Around him stand
The loved companions in his hours of pleasure;
Now with their hearts attuned to sorrow's measure—
  A ministering band:
They soothe the pains affection may not heal,
And blunt his dying pangs in those they feel.

'Tis on the wave,
Amid that crowded, dismal, lonely prison,
When hundreds from the ship's strained ribs have risen
  To darkness and the grave;
That deepest horrors burst upon the soul,
And wild despair o'ermasters all control.

Athwart the main,
An ocean-barrier to man's world surrounding,
And his frail ark from every blow rebounding,
  As surely with the strain
She settles deeper in her watery tomb,
Death shrouds the victim with his darkest gloom.

Hope casts no ray
Across the vast expanse of mountain-billows:
The sounding surge which every moment pillows
  Still lower on her way
That parting hulk in silence and in night,
Drowns, in its roar, the hundred shrieks of fright.

One awful hour,
And to the fathomless abyss descending,
With winds and waves their wildest discord blending,
  No trace will evermore
Reveal the secrets of that living grave,
Where Death confronts the beautiful and brave.

Oh! it is there
That fitly is he named the King of Terrors;
Elsewhere man dies in hope that some kind bearers,
   Some spirits of earth or air,
Will carry sad memorials to bless
The mourning objects of his tenderness.

   But who shall tell
The anxious watchers o'er each darkening morrow,
That dreaded tale to fill their cup of sorrow?
   Who bear the mute farewell?
Alas! Annihilation rears her head—
He dies—and, with him, all around is dead!

THE

ANNIVERSARY OF MARRIAGE.

"One shall be taken, and the other left."

I.

YEARS roll their course—but none so sad as this,
Has ever marked my pilgrimage on earth;
This day, the dear remembrancer of bliss,
Till now more joyous than the date of birth,
Brings, in the fullness, to my soul its dearth—
Paints the dread contrast with life's happiest hours,
When cheered by her, the angel of my hearth,
The idol of a heart where anguish lowers—
Then life's perennial bloom was ever strewn with flowers.

II.

But ah! no more, for me no more that dawn
Which ushers in another welcomed year;
The one that ever gladdened it is gone
To add refulgence in a holier sphere—
Forth from my widowed couch, alone, I rear
On the scathed altar of departed joys,
Whence, late, united breathings rose in prayer,
My orisons to Him, whose bolt destroys
In wisdom, all of earth that heaven's pure love alloys.

83

III.

Father Supreme! thus lowly in the dust,
Where thou hast stretched my agonizèd frame
Broken and crushed, my deep, unfalt'ring trust
Can yet thy mercy and thy love proclaim;
With praises magnify thy sacred name
From the dark caverns of my soul's distress—
For thou, O God! art good—e'en now the same,
In boundless love and justice not the less
That from thy hand I drink the cup of bitterness.

IV.

Shall I repine, and with a murm'ring heart
Receive thy direst dispensation now?
Ah! no; I've known Thee ever what thou art,
The blest consoler in each earthly wo,—
All, all is thine; if, 'mid the ceaseless flow
Of gifts unnumbered from that bounteous hand,
In wisdom thou hast dealt this heaviest blow,
It is that she, my loved, lost one, may stand
With kindred round thy throne in heaven's seraphic band.

V.

Shall I, the meanest of its sons, rebel,
When, in the record of thy wondrous ways
And equal dealings, holy penmen tell
Of saints and prophets proved in former days—
Of righteous Job, focus of all the rays
That Satan's wrath could pour on helpless man,
Yet from that trial, for thy greater praise,
More rich and honored than his course began,
He came, prepared to live and lengthen out life's span.

8 *

VI.

Shall I dare murmur when I read of Him,
Thy Son, the Saviour of this world of wo,
Thine *outward* Presence, mangled limb by limb,
With scornèd front and desecrated brow—
Alone, abandoned e'en by Thee, to show,
In life's accumulated ills, how sure
An Arm of Power, encircling hell below,
Can shield untouched the humble and the pure—
How far the God can reach, how much the man endure.

VII.

Oh! have I not, with that all perfect One,
Wept through the gloom of night's funereal pall,
Watched in the agony of soul alone,
Drank to the dregs the wormwood and the gall?
Have I not known, in verity, the fall
Of sweat, as 'twere great drops of my heart's gore?
Have I not felt the loss of more than all
That earth beside can yield from richest store,
The star, the light of life, the love that gilt it o'er?

VIII.

Yet, shall I murmur? No! I bless the rod,
Which, chastening, weans me from this lower sphere,
Brings to my sense the presence of a God,
With whom to dwell is to be alien here—
Renews my strength to run that high career
Whose aim's Eternal Life—whose goal is bliss—
Whose staff, humility—whose guide, the fear
Of Thee, the one omnipotent—I kiss
Thy rod that gives the blow—I bless thee most for this.

IX.

For well I know that in affliction's hour
Thine is the empire, thine the ruling sway—
Within its furnace every other power,
Which binds rebellious man, consumes away;
Not one among th' angelic host that pray
Before thy throne, but who, in former years,
Hath passed this portal to the realms of day;
Has borne, in trial, all our doubts and fears,
Has felt the anguished heart, and wept the scalding tears.

X.

Well, too, I know that, though a worthless worm
In groveling bondage to sin's mortal stain,
With a high hand and an outstretchèd arm,
Thou, Father of Eternity! wilt deign
To clasp in mercy's fold a son again—
That wisdom infinite, that boundless power,
Are freely proffered to restore thy reign—
Oh! shall I shun adversity's brief hour,
And weigh the ills of Time with Life forevermore?

XI.

If to thy glory I may consecrate,
While breath remains, a dedicated soul,
What thou hast given of grace and strength, prostrate
In humble service to thy loved control—
If, while o'er me the circling seasons roll,
I stand, a living witness of Thy name,
Then shall my wishes reach their loftiest goal—
What, to the glorious prize, were wealth or fame!
What all the martyr's pangs—the life-long badge of shame!

XII.

Thus, dearest Father, from thy stricken child,
Now bowed in sorrow, comes the song of praise;
Heaven's law is just, though we, by sin defiled,
Fail to unfold the wisdom of thy ways—
Preserve me still, that all my future days
May know no object but to honor Thee—
To Thee, to Thee, in gratitude, I raise
The prayer of faith—oh! may its guerdon be
My sure defence through Time—its hope, Eternity.

SILENT WORSHIP.

1 KINGS XIX. 11–13.

O N Horeb's brow the prophet stood,[29]
   To hold communion with his God,
When, with tremendous rush, the wind came roaring,
And shivered mountains while he bent adoring:
     Hurled rifted rocks in air,
       Crashed through the woods,
       Upheaved the floods;
     But yet He was not there!

     The earthquake shook his slippery stand,
     And scattered ruin o'er the land;
Tossed the rent ground like foam upon the billow,
And rocked huge acres o'er their granite pillow:
     Aghast the startled seer,
       As low he knelt,
       Too surely felt
     Jehovah was not there!

     Then burst the subterranean fire,
     To him the world's funereal pyre;

Through countless seams its lava-streams descending,
Till, land and sea in primal chaos blending,
  He wept o'er Nature's bier;
   Yet wept he more,
   That, 'mid the roar,
  His Saviour was not there.

  He ceased: a still, small voice, at last,
  Its gentle whisper through him passed;
He knew the Power, whose light, itself revealing,
Breaks in a flood upon the world of feeling:
  Then, veiled in secret prayer,
   Serene and still,
   Prostrate his will,
  God communed with him there!

LINES

WRITTEN ON HEARING OF THE DEATH OF CHIEF
JUSTICE MARSHALL.

THE dust of common men descends to earth,
   In death unnoticed, as unknown in birth,
E'en like the wave, a few short moments tossed
To brief existence, sinks, forever lost;
But oh! how vast the void one giant mind,
Torn from its earthly prison, leaves behind!
Millions are born to feed the ignoble dearth,
But ages slowly give a sage to earth.

And such as thou! O, how unlike the great,
Whose daring deeds are curses to a state!
How far removed thy worth from vulgar gaze,
From tinseled fame, or sycophantic praise!
How pure thy life, how silently sublime
The works that herald thee to latest time!
While, with the gaudy blaze of scenic art,
A hero's actions captivate the heart,
Till calmer reason's light reveals to view
The meteor fame distorted and untrue,

Thy name, O Marshall! like some work divine
Of Rome's great artist, bends not to decline;
Though time and age may soften down each trace,
And sombre darkness moulder o'er its grace,
Still, year on year but stamps increasing worth,
As distance dims the era of its birth.
Thus, on the tablet of thy country's page,
Thy works will brighten with each passing age,
Thy words become the oracles of lore,
Where wisdom speaks in light forevermore.
Yet oh! while thus with triumph we survey
The matchless glory of thy future day,
While young Columbia, prouder of thy fame
Than all that clusters round each living name,
Basks in the splendor of thy mental worth,
She mourns, alas! her prophet snatched from earth.
Where hath his mantle fallen? from whom below
Shall all of learning, genius, wisdom flow?
Where shall she seek for virtue nobly joined
With the bright wonders of immortal mind?
Where look for toil unceasing in her cause,
To build on truth the pile of human laws?
Or where, like his, a soul, whose eagle eye
May pierce at once the web of sophistry,
Strip from the subtlest art its veil away,
And cast on latent guilt the light of day?
But where, oh! where that firm, unflinching brow,
Through storms of state, so dearly needed now?
Where may she seek that moral courage, drawn
From hearts like his, who fought with freedom's dawn,
That godlike rectitude, that spotless life,
Above all value in this world of strife,
Which, joined to stern authority, remove
The mountain passions to a sea of love,

Calm down the swell of stormy faction's wave,
And save a state, when nought beside can save.
Oh! last of all the race—for none remain
Of those whose virtue bade young freedom reign;
Of all that noble band, who paved the way
To reason's perfect light and equal sway,
Whose souls united gave the wond'ring earth
That sacred charter of their country's birth
And man's regeneration—all have passed,
And thou with them, the greatest and the last.
The greatest thou; for though by others framed,
From thee that charter more than language claimed:
To thee Columbia owes its wondrous power
To quell the storms of faction's angry hour;
Thine is the glory of its sovereign sway
O'er states whom only reason bids obey,
O'er hearts united for their country's cause,
And bound by thee in truth's eternal laws.
Where hath thy mantle fallen? to whom is given
A magic influence less of earth than heaven?
To whom thy virtue now, so rarely known,
Where dark intrigue pollutes a nation's throne?[30]
Alas! the rolling years will pass along,
And host on host may swell th' ambitious throng,
Heroes will rise to dazzle and to blind,
And statesmen rule republics undermined;
But such as thee mankind may seek in vain,
"We shall not look upon thy like again."

9

WAR.

I.

AGAIN the tocsin sounds; the trumpet's blast
Rings through the earth its stirring call to arms,
Breaks up the slumbers of the peaceful past,
And shakes a prospering world with dread alarms:
Again Bellona guides, with awful charms,
The crushing progress of her crimson car
O'er maddened hearts and quivering human forms:
Pride, Hatred, Rage, Despair, malignant jar
By turns the minds of men, and Hell is loosed with War.

II.

On Europe's teeming fields and smiling plains,
Rich with the harvests of her forty years,
Enthroned supreme, the dark Destroyer reigns,
To drench her soil anew with blood and tears:
The epoch now, whose lurid dawn appears
With horrid portents o'er her darkened sky,
Those signs of widest desolation wears,
That lowered when, kindled at Gaul's battle-cry,
Her nations all were joined in dreadful rivalry.

III.

Millions of men, her flower, in manhood's prime,
May die in anguish at each other's hands;
And ah! the millions more, unstained by crime,
Whose tears will flow upon her bloody sands!
Her lofty cities sacked by hostile bands;
Her wealth, her commerce, sunk in ocean's wave:
Her peaceful strength transferred to other lands;
Her sons the tenants of an early grave;
These are the fruits of war, and all it ever gave.

IV.

That rolling cycle comes to earth again,
When Folly, Crime, and Madness rule the hour:
Too high the joys which Peace, with gentle reign,
Hath brought to nations as her heavenly dower:
False Honor spurns her ever-spreading power;
Ambition trails her symbols in the dust:
Man, restless, rushes from her roseate bower,
Where safety circles his unfaltering trust,
To brave the certain ills of anarchy and lust.

V.

What though for Justice spring his glittering sword!
For Freedom, ring th' exulting battle-cry!
For meek Religion, blood in seas be poured!
For glory's meed, his countless squadrons die!
Has not earth heard that oft-repeated lie
Enough to learn the worthlessness of war?
Is not, in woes alone, the history
Of every contest writ, on every shore,
Since Cain's first murder stained her virgin soil with gore.

VI.

Shall she repeat, on Europe's cultured plains,
The last great drama of her crimsoned page,
To feel, at length, that some Napoleon reigns,
The demon-despot of a brutal age?
That war, which fed, must crush his boundless rage,
And all her labors end where they began?
That nations, drained, exhausted, vainly wage
The horrid combat between man and man?
Have all her sufferings taught no wiser, better plan?

VII.

Shall tyrants frame communities to share
Of one, or wise or weak, the weal or wo?
Shall statesmen still their fettered country bear
To cast its fortunes on a desperate throw,
And risk all hopes in war's uncertain blow?
Must men be ever chained to feel and fight
The banded puppets of Ambition's show?
Must patriot folly drown all sense of right?
Then truly Earth is yet in her primeval night.

VIII.

What hope had Virtue here, or gentle Peace,
Her sweet concomitant, were this a scene
Not ended soon by welcome Death's release,
While stern Oppression clouds its silvery sheen?
Though skies are bright, and smiling landscapes green,
In full luxuriance pouring forth their store;
What, if the conqueror tread this fair terrene,
To drench its flowery fields with human gore,
But kindred Hell were Earth, without that happier shore?

IX.

Alas! too surely of a fallen race
Is ceaseless war th' unanswerable seal!
To men redeemed by Heaven-appointed grace,
Its mission here is not to cause, but heal,
The thousand ills which suffering brethren feel.
How wide the contrast, when a world is swayed
By airy trifles, pretexts scarcely real,
For mortal strife to draw the glittering blade,
And march, the tools of Power, in serried bands arrayed!

X.

What were the pleasures of a scene like this,
With man th' eternal habitant, as now
A selfish foeman to his neighbor's bliss—
Nor less his own—through wickedness and wo?
The fabled torturers in realms below
Were impotent of ill to human sway:
Remove Death's signet from his iron brow,
Renew his lease within this house of clay,
And fiends, as types of men, would shrink with wild dismay!

XI.

Does he not vainly hope for future heaven,
Who bears the hell of hatred in his heart;
Asks of a Father's love to be forgiven,
Yet plays on earth the fratricidal part,
Where Lust and Folly rule its every start?
A true descendant of the first-born Cain,
The causeless murderer, drilled by *nicer* art,
As doomed a wanderer o'er her fair domain,
To bring unnumbered woes where'er he treads the plain.

9 *

XII.

Shall nations never sheathe th' avenging sword,
And learn to trust its doubtful chance no more?
Alas! fulfilment of the prophet's word
Scarce nearer seems than ever yet before!
The grim portents of universal war,
Masked in profession of His holy name,
Whose life, and deeds, and heavenly language, bore
The glorious anthem sounded when He came,
Hang o'er a trembling world, to burst with quenchless flame.

XIII.

His doctrine taught Earth's erring child of sin
The truth enforced on each historic page,
That Heaven's loved sway is only known within,
Through bloodless war with man's unhallowed rage;
That, leaving all, his ransomed soul must wage
A contest ended but with Nature's life;
A ceaseless fight with self, through every stage
Of fierce rebellion in that nature rife,
Till, meekly bowed like Him, submission crowns the strife.

XIV.

When born anew, through God's redeeming gift,
The creature learns his law of boundless love,
Then, nor till then, may hopes eternal lift
Their raptured reach to realms of peace above.
Here lust, and hate, and pride, and passion prove
Destruction's reign o'er Justice, Truth, and Right:
These, nor their willing slaves, can ever move
Beyond the gloom of earth's Cimmerian night;
For Heaven is meekness, joy, and purity, and light!

NOTES.

NOTES.

NOTE 1. PAGE 10.

" The blood-stained victor's son."

THE founder of Pennsylvania was educated by his father, Admiral Penn, in all the accomplishments at that time deemed necessary for the position he was destined to fill. The title of Lord Weymouth, with an elevation to the peerage, had been tendered, which would have descended to William Penn. The thorough acquaintance with arms would, of course, be considered important as a branch of training. In Paris, a sudden encounter proved him an accomplished swordsman.

NOTE 2. PAGE 10.

" Made captives of their swarthy tribes who roam,
For horrid fate in unknown climes abroad."

The practice of kidnapping the natives had been extensively carried on,—especially, in earlier periods, by the Portuguese. Gaspar Cortereal managed at one time to get fifty or more on board his vessel, whom he sold as slaves. John de Verazzano, of Florence, with a French crew, had one of these, in imminent danger of drowning, rescued by the natives,—whom they delivered to him with every token of kindness and good-will. In return, his boat was sent ashore at another place with twenty men. "They penetrated into the country about six miles. The people fled from them in fear. By a careful search they discovered, concealed in the high grass, an old woman heavily laden. She bore upon her shoulders two infants, and behind her neck a little boy, eight years old. In her company was a young squaw, about eighteen years of age. When the Frenchmen approached them, they shrieked aloud, and made significant gestures to the men who had returned to the woods. To allay their fears, the visitors offered them provisions, which the old woman gratefully received, but the younger one spurned from her. Everything which they offered this young and beautiful damsel of the forest, she disdainfully threw upon the ground. She was too high-spirited to allow herself to be placed under any obligations to these pale-faced strangers. They ought to have treated these two unprotected, helpless females with kindness, and then suffered them to depart. But, instead of this, these chivalrous Frenchmen cruelly stole from the old woman the boy that was under her care, and then tried to carry off the girl. But she screamed so loud, and resisted so violently, that they saw it would be impossible to get her through the woods to the boat. They had to content themselves with the little child, whom they carried off with the intention of taking to France." Dunna-conna, a native king, was kidnapped by Cartier on the St. Lawrence River, and carried to France. The practice was not unfrequent throughout the sixteenth century; so that the Indians were rendered in some vicinities, and justly so, very suspicious of all white men.

NOTE 3. PAGE 11.

> "*A deed begun,*
> *Man, unregenerate, pardoned ne'er before,*
> *But washed its blackness out with seas of human gore.*"

The sentence of our Saviour, "Go, and sin no more," is in strong contrast with the ten years' Trojan war, caused by the faithlessness of a woman to her marriage vows."

NOTE 4. PAGE 12.

> "*These the two wings, the angel wings that bear*
> *The soul, redeemed from earth, to reach its heavenly*
> *sphere.*"

The idea is taken from the "Imitation of Christ," by Thomas A'Kempis.

NOTE 5. PAGE 12.

> "*And the spoiler's art,*
> *Which Rome and Spain had grafted on the chart*
> *Of Europe's claim to heathen lands, destroyed,*"

The claim of the Pope, as head of Christendom, to grant the lands of heathen was necessarily transferred to Henry VIII., when the bond was broken between them. Charles II., his successor, granted to William Penn the province of Pennsylvania in lieu of paying a debt due his father for services; more especially "in that signal battle and victory fought and obtained against the Dutch fleet, commanded by the Heer Van Opdam, in the year 1665." None doubted the title thus granted, but Penn's sense of justice required him to respect the right of the natives as much as if there were no other claim. It is related of him, that having broached this idea in a conversation with the king, the latter, in sur-prise, exclaimed, "Why, man, you have already bought of me." "True," was the reply, "but I am to agree also with them." As an illustration of his policy, tradition also relates, that, in a treaty for land with the natives, the latter conceived themselves the victims of a hard bargain, and exhibited signs of discontent. Penn's watchful sagacity perceived it, and he had them brought before him to learn its cause. His advisers insisted on the necessity of holding the party to their solemn contract. They had sold, and if they could at pleasure annul it, the precedent would be established for the overthrow of all land titles. Penn, however, persisted, and the result was that he could administer as salutary a lesson as Canute to his courtiers. "See," said he, "those children of the forest, whom a little christian patience, with a few more matchcoats and blankets, have sent away our friends. Your policy would have caused a feeling of bitterness, which, in all probability, would have led to acts of revenge, the consequence of which might have been wars and fighting."

NOTE 6. PAGE 13.

"*Conscience achieved its freedom from the chains*
Of human law," *&c.*

The right had before been advocated, but scarcely established, by Roger Williams and others.

NOTE 7. PAGE 14.

"*The mart whence noisome odors ever rise,*
Where he had left a bank of green declivities."

The plan of the Proprietor was to leave the space east of Front Street open to the river. The river bank is high and nearly uniform, and had his plan been fully carried out, Philadelphia might have been, in its regularity and beauty of design, the finest city in the world.

NOTE 8. PAGE 14.

" The germs were there of this prodigious fruit,—
The frame of what we since have realized."

To use the language of a modern observer* :—"In the early constitutions of Pennsylvania are to be found the distinct annunciation of every great principle; the germ, if not the development of every valuable improvement in government or legislation, which has been introduced into the political systems of more modern epochs."

NOTE 9. PAGE 16.

" Nor church nor priestly power may claim, by law,
O'er human conscience more that dread control."

" No religious test shall ever be required as a qualification to any office or public trust under the United States."

" Congress shall make no law respecting an establishment of religion, or prohibiting the free exercise thereof."—*United States Constitution.*

" All men have a natural and indefeasible right to worship Almighty God according to the dictates of their own consciences; no man can of right be compelled to attend, erect, or support any place of worship, or to maintain any ministry against his consent: no human authority can, in any case whatever, control or interfere with the rights of conscience; and no preference shall ever be given, by law, to any religious establishments or modes of worship."—*Constitution of Pennsylvania, Art. IX., Sect. III.*

---

* T. J. Wharton. See Watson's Annals, i. 314, quoted in Janney's Life of Penn, p. 182.

10

Note 10. Page 16.

" *The yielding barriers prove how strong the net that's spun.*"

The commonwealth of Pennsylvania was established, and has carefully been continued, on the principle that "Almighty God is alone lord of conscience." In latter years we have found indications multiplying, which point to an invasion of this great prerogative. A specimen of the tendency may be cited from the Act of May 9, 1866, incorporating the "Lincoln Institution," the managers and council whereof, by Section 4, may take under guardianship:— " *Secondly.* White boys and youths, between the age of twelve and twenty-one years, who *may be committed to the care* of the said managers and council by any *judge of the Supreme Court of Pennsylvania,* or of the *District Court of the city and county of Philadelphia,* or of the *Court of Common Pleas of the city and county of Philadelphia,* on account of vagrancy, or the exposure, or neglect, or abandonment of said boys, or youths, by their parents, or parent, guardians, or other persons having custody thereof."

" The inmates shall, in all cases, have respect for the faith of the Protestant Episcopal Church of the United States, and submit to the religious exercises of the household, which shall *always be in accordance with the belief of that church; and all children received, under twelve years of age, shall be trained in that faith.*"

Note 11. Page 18.

" *Who, in the constant strife of factions, reads*
   Bright promise for a country," *&c.*

I clip the following from the day's gazette. The word " Central" may be fairly considered superfluous :—

" PEACE IN CENTRAL AMERICA.—' The five republics of

Central America are at peace; consequently, there is no news from there.' We find the foregoing in the telegraphic despatches of yesterday. Brief as it is, and pointless as it appears to be, it is nevertheless a very suggestive paragraph. It is unfortunately true that almost from the day of the independence of these Central American republics, almost the only news that we have had from there have been accounts of revolutions and counter-revolutions, of pronunciamentos and plans, and wars growing out of these never-ending disturbances. Hence it is that we are informed by this despatch that, no wars or revolutions being on hand in Central America, there is no news to send; but if this tranquil condition of affairs shall continue for any length of time, as we hope it may, we shall soon have the most agreeable news of progress and prosperity and happiness, and all that results from the blessed reign of peace, where the country is fertile, and the people free."

Note 12. Page 20.

"*Law's unimpeded reign,*
By moral force, would draw the stranger's praise
At scenes so foreign to his country's ways."

Few things excited the astonishment of foreigners more than the quiet obedience to law which characterized the citizen, and the entire absence of any visible controlling force. Peter S. Duponceau, the only revolutionary relic I have any vivid remembrance of, says, in his Preface to the "Brief View of the Constitution":—

"When differences have arisen between the general and the state governments, conciliation has been found the most effectual means of settling them The constitution itself is the result of compromise, and is best preserved by the same means by which it has been obtained. May Heaven avert, for many ages, the fatal period when our differences shall have to be settled by brutal force! Between powers so nicely balanced, a collision is ever to be dreaded.

"An intelligent foreigner, after perusing these sheets, made the following remark: 'Your constitution was made for a *virtuous people;* but it will not suit any other.' Let us, then, continue to be virtuous, and we may hope to be long united, happy and free."

NOTE 13. PAGE 26.

> " *Must I obey,*
> *Or follow Him, the true, eternal way,*
> *And love them—feed them?*"

Blackstone, in his Commentaries, states that "it is held by all the writers on the law of nature and nations, that the right of making war, which *by nature subsisted in every individual,* is given up by all private persons that enter into society, and is vested in the sovereign power." Such a foundation for the right assumed, to compel the citizen to fight, has especial relevancy to my condition. My ancestors and their friends settled this section of country; they laid the foundation of its polity on the rights of conscience. The world is sufficiently informed that, like the early christians, they testified against war as contrary to christianity. "I am a christian, and cannot fight," was the answer of many in the earlier periods, when drafted for Roman armies. In the contract, therefore, between me and the government, I may deny its claim *to shoot me as a deserter* for refusing to serve, because I do not believe that the right, as a follower of Christ, subsists to make war; not claiming it myself, I have not given it to the government. Again, the constitution of my state declares, that I "shall not be compelled to bear arms, but shall *pay an equivalent* for personal service." It is pleasing to find a consciousness of this in the answers of our public functionaries to a committee sent to Washington with an address from the Yearly Meeting of Friends, held at Philadelphia, as appears by the following extract from their report :—

"The Address was read to each by one of our number, and a copy handed to them; also, a copy left for each one of the Secretaries who were not in Washington.

"Our interviews with the President and cabinet were of a very satisfactory and interesting character.

"After the object of our visit was stated by one of the committee, and the reading and presentation of the Address to the President, he responded thereto, thanking us and those we represented for this evidence of our regard for our lamented President, Abraham Lincoln, and sympathy for his loss, and expressed his desire to be guided by Divine Wisdom in the discharge of the great responsibilities which had so unexpectedly devolved upon him. He said he was no sectarian; that his religion would span the universe, like the bow resting upon one part of the horizon, and extending to the other; that he was well acquainted with the views of his predecessor, and should endeavor to carry them out, and we might rest assured that a like regard for conscientious scruples, which had been extended to us by our late President, it would be his pleasure to extend in future as occasion required. We took our leave of him under a feeling of solemnity, after an impressive prayer by one of our number.

"Very impressive was our interview with the Secretary of War, Edwin M. Stanton, who said, 'I am deeply impressed by your visit, and affected by the sympathy expressed by you and your Society in the beautiful Address, in the loss we have sustained, as you say, by violence, of our President,

10 *   H

Abraham Lincoln. Your appreciation of his character is just. Having been closely associated with him for several years, I know that no appeal was made to his heart, which he did not respond to by acts of kindness and sympathy. He and myself felt that, unless we recognized conscientious religious scruples, we could not expect the blessing of Heaven.' He expressed with much tenderness his satisfaction with our visit, and near the conclusion said, 'I beseech you that prayers may be offered up for us by you and all christian denominations. We know what has passed, but we know not what may be in the future. Our worthy President is gone to rest from his labors, and my desire is, that when my time comes, whether my life may be taken by violence or otherwise, I also may be prepared. by doing my duty, to enter into rest.'

"The Secretary of State, William H. Seward, was in his room, he not having recovered from his wounds; but hearing of our mission in Washington, said he wanted us to come, one by one, and take him by the hand, though he should not be able to converse with us. This we did, with a few words of sympathetic greeting, leaving with him a copy of the Address, with which he expressed his satisfaction."

NOTE 14. PAGE 26.

"A petty trespass—nay, a less than wrong,
May arm them all war's dreadful course to run."

The idea in the first part of this stanza was suggested by a paragraph from one of Daniel Webster's speeches. The trial of Alexander McLeod, in the state of New York, some thirty years ago, and the serious dilemma we were placed in by the want of Federal power to comply with the demand of the British government, furnishes a case such as is alluded to in the lines following. Had he been punished as a mur-

derer for an act avowed as done by its authority, it is prob-
able that, according to the custom, the two nations would
have been declared at war.   Every man, therefore, the world
over, subject to the British government, would have been
the personal foe of every citizen of the United States, bound
to destroy his property and life, and forbidden to extend him
aid or comfort under the heaviest penalties.   Such is the
law of war.

Note 15.   Page 27.

" I, like the Persian, may refuse control."

Otanes, who, according to Herodotus in his Thalia, made
a condition with his co-conspirators, that no one of them
(who were about to choose a king from their number) should
ever reign over him or any of his posterity.

Note 16.   Page 29.

" Each party claims the law, and calls to God,
As erst in battle's wage, for victory."

The trial by wager of battle "seems to have owed its
original (says Blackstone in his Commentaries) to the military spirit of our ancestors, joined to a superstitious frame
of mind : it being in the nature of an appeal to Providence,
under an apprehension and hope (however presumptuous
and unwarrantable) that Heaven would give the victory to
him who had the right.   The decision of suits by this appeal
to the God of battles is by some said to have been invented
by the Burgundi, one of the northern or German clans that
planted themselves in Gaul."

"The trial was introduced into England among other
Norman customs by William the Conqueror, but was only
used in three cases—one military, one criminal, and the
third civil.   The first in the court-martial, or court of

chivalry and honor; the second in appeals of felony, of which we shall speak in the next book; and the third upon issue joined in a writ of right, the last and most solemn decision of real property."

Note 17. Page 30.

" *The rex de facto doctrine may anew*
   Guide through the tangled web allegiance draws;
   Though rose be white or red, not ours to brave the laws."

During the wars between the houses of York and Lancaster, the respective badges of which were the white and red rose, hence called the wars of the roses, from the necessity of the case, the acts of the party in power for the time were recognized. Each claiming its own king as rex de jure, while obliged to acknowledge the other as rex de facto during its possession of the sovereign power. The principle appears now to be universally acknowledged.

Note 18. Page 35.

" *Or shall the empire prove another lease*
   For life or years—another deluge be
   Reserved, to burst again from dread futurity?

The allusion here is to the words attributed to Louis XV.: "After me the deluge." The first Napoleon held what may be termed a lease for years, since he abdicated in favor of Napoleon II., who, as the present is Napoleon III., if he reigned at all, must have done so till death. I clip, while writing, the following paragraph from the daily newspaper, as an illustration of what I have endeavored to portray in the preceding few stanzas:—

"The number of peace treaties which have been signed in the last two hundred years is said to be seven thousand two hundred and five; and it is also a remarkable fact that each of these treaties begins with the statement that the peace hereby declared shall be enduring and last forever."

NOTE 19. PAGE 37.

" We here have felt how much it thus behooved
To guard from every ill—to foster worth beloved."

It was held by the Supreme Court of the United States, that the charter granted by the British crown to the trustees of Dartmouth College, in New Hampshire, in the year 1769, is a contract within the meaning of that clause of the constitution of the United States (Art. I., Sect. 10), which declares that no state shall make any law impairing the obligation of contracts; and this charter was not dissolved by the revolution; and that a law of the state altering the charter in a material respect, without the consent of the corporation, was unconstitutional and void.

In 1835 the Legislature of Pennsylvania passed an Act to authorize its citizens to vote on the expediency of electing delegates, who were to submit amendments to the state constitution, but with no other powers. This resulted in a majority of 3000, out of 150,000 votes cast, for the proposed course. The number of votes cast for the office of governor of the state (for the term of three years) was 50,000 more than on the question, "For" or "against" a convention. These delegates were duly elected, sat, and presented a new constitution, which was accordingly voted for, and adopted by a majority of less than 1500; and at the same time 30,000 more votes were cast for the office of governor than on this vital question.

One of the features of the new constitution was a change in the judicial tenure from life, during good behaviour, to a term of years, and, instead of executive appointment, the office was made elective by the people. The Chief Justice of Pennsylvania was, by the schedule appended to the instrument, to be dispossessed in about seven or eight years, and the longest period assigned therein was fifteen years. He had sat on the bench twenty-two years and upwards, was acknowledged by all competent to decide as the ablest and most suitable for his high office; and his decisions are models of legal terseness and acumen. Having been commissioned during life, as far as human foresight might penetrate, he naturally supposed his salary could be relied on, and either neglected or was unable to provide for so unlooked-for a blast. To obtain, therefore, the benefit of the longest period in the schedule, he resigned, and was at once re-commissioned by the governor. I was present when the commission was read in court, and I felt, with all capable of right feeling, the degradation, the humiliation of the act. The old ostracism of Greece seemed revived, but that was from jealousy; here it was a deliberate outrage upon consistency and right. If the grant to a corporation cannot be affected by a total revolution in government, I am at a loss to understand how that to an individual can be invaded and destroyed by what politicians call " the majority of the people," in defiance of constitutional provisions."

Note 20. Page 37.
"As each Olympiad its game renews."

" The Greeks computed their time by the celebrated era of the Olympiads, which date from the year 776 B. C., being the year in which Coræbus was successful at the Olympic games. This era differed from all others in being reckoned by periods of four years instead of single years. Each period of four years was called an *Olympiad*."—*Encyclopædia Americana.*

NOTE 21. PAGE 39.

" Will millions stake their all, and madly spurn
Blessings and gifts, earth's choicest boons among,
Without a cause—aye!—grievances—and strong?

This echoes the sentiment in the Declaration of Independence, that "all experience hath shown that mankind are more disposed to suffer, while evils are sufferable, than to right themselves by abolishing the forms to which they are accustomed."

NOTE 22. PAGE 41.

" Typed well in him whose mad ambition stole
Celestial fire," &c.

Prometheus—in fabulous history—whom Jupiter caused, for having stolen fire from heaven, to be chained by Vulcan on a rock of the Caucasus, where his liver, which was renewed each night, was gnawed every day by an eagle. Various have been the interpretations of this celebrated myth. The eagle was especially the companion, and sometimes type, of Jupiter, and may well represent the voice which reasons with us in the cool of the day on our nocturnal renewals of forbidden pleasures.

NOTE 23. PAGE 44.

"How well Themistocles this truth was taught!"

"Themistocles, having one day declared to the general assembly, that he had thought of an expedient which was very salutary to Athens, but ought to be kept secret, he was ordered to communicate it to Aristides only, and abide by his judgment of it. Accordingly, he told him, his project was to burn the whole fleet of the confederates; by which means the Athenians would be raised to the sovereignty of all Greece. Aristides then returned to the assembly, and acquainted the Athenians, 'That nothing could be more advantageous than the project of Themistocles, nor anything more unjust.' And, upon his report of the matter, they commanded Themistocles to give over all thoughts of it. Such regard had that people for justice, and so much confidence in the integrity of Aristides."—*Plutarch, Life of Themistocles.*

NOTE 24. PAGE 49.

" Such is the outline—stripped of honied phrase."

As a specimen of the modern German and French Lives of Jesus, take the following from Ernest Rénan, page 361 :—

"At Bethany there happened an event, which seems to have exercised an important influence on the end of His career. Wearied out with the ill success of the kingdom of God at the capital of the country, the friends of Jesus longed for some great miracle, which should give a shock to its incredulity. And the resurrection of a person well known at Jerusalem seemed to be just what was wanted. Now we must remember that the first condition of a true criticism is to comprehend the differences that characterize different epochs, and to overcome the instinctive feelings of repugnance which are sure to arise in minds of a purely intellectual culture. We must remember also that, in this impure and oppressive atmosphere of Jerusalem, Jesus was no longer himself. His conscience, from the fault of others and not his own, had lost something of its original transparent clearness. In despair,—driven (as it were) to bay,—he was no longer his own master. His mission pressed heavily upon him, and at length he gave way and floated down the stream. . . . . We are, on the whole, inclined to believe that at Bethany some real event or other happened, which was regarded as a resurrection. Rumor had already attributed to Jesus two or three miracles of this kind. The family

at Bethany may, without much reflection, have been induced
to lend themselves to an act fraught with such eventful
issues. Jesus was adored among them.   Lazarus, it seems,
had been sick ; and it was a message from the anxious sisters
which had brought Jesus back from Parǽa.   The joy of
seeing him again may have restored Lazarus to life ; or it
may be that an eagerness to stop the mouths of cavilers
against the divine mission of their friend drove those warm
temperaments beyond all bounds.   And so, perhaps, Lazarus—pale from the effects of his illness—allowed himself to
be swathed like a corpse, and placed in the family tomb.
These tombs were extensive chambers hollowed out of the
rock, and the squared entrance was closed by a huge stone.
Martha and Mary went forth to meet Jesus, and, without
entering the village, conducted him to the cavern. . . . .
Jesus—we speak still under the hypothesis above suggested—
desired once more to see him whom he had loved; and the
stone being rolled away, Lazarus issued forth 'bound with
grave-clothes, and his face bound about with a napkin.'   The
apparition would naturally be regarded by every one as a
resurrection.   For faith knows no law, &c."

NOTE 25.   PAGE 55.

"Deprived of every sense but touch, its ray
Will reach in converse from that inner shrine."

Alluding to the case of Laura Bridgman, a pupil of the
Perkins Institution for the Blind, under the tuition of Dr.
Howe, in Massachusetts, taken into it at eight years of age,
and instructed with such success as to be able to communicate her ideas, and to receive, to a great extent, an education
like others.   Her condition, given in the report made at the
end of the year, is this, having been the same from birth :—

" It has been ascertained, beyond the possibility of doubt,

11

that she cannot see a ray of light, cannot hear the least
sound, and never exercises the sense of smell, if she has
any. Thus her mind dwells in darkness and stillness as
profound as that of a closed tomb at midnight."

Note 26.   Page 57.

"A world-wide fame like Penn's has found a jilt.
No Muse, in hist'ry's brilliant half romance."

The "half romance" of Macaulay's History of England,
if not justified fully by his perversion of plain facts in treat-
ing such well-known characters as William Penn, the Duke
of Marlborough, James II., and others, against whom party
feeling seems to have blinded historical judgment, may be
warranted by his own notions of what history should be.
In an essay on the subject in the Edinburgh Review for
1828, he says:

"If a man, such as we are supposing, should write the
history of England, he would assuredly not omit the battles,
the sieges, the negotiations, the seditions, the ministerial
changes. But with these he would intersperse the details
which are the *charm of historical romances.* At Lincoln
Cathedral there is a beautiful painted window, which was
made by an apprentice out of the pieces of glass which had
been rejected by his master. It is so far superior to every
other in the church, that, according to the tradition, the
vanquished artist killed himself from mortification. Sir
Walter Scott, in the same manner, has used those fragments
of truth which historians have scornfully thrown behind
them, in a manner which may well excite their envy. He
has constructed out of their gleanings works which, even
considered as histories, are scarcely less valuable than theirs.
But a truly great historian would reclaim those materials
which the novelist has appropriated. The history of the

government and the history of the people would be exhibited in that mode, in which alone they can be exhibited justly, in inseparable conjunction and intermixture. We should not then have to look for the wars and votes of the Puritans in Clarendon, and for their phraseology in Old Mortality; for one-half of King James in Hume, and for the other half in the Fortunes of Nigel."

M. de Lamartine meeting M. Alexander Dumas soon after the publication of the History of the Girondins, inquired anxiously of the famous romance-writer if he had read it. "Oui; c'est superbe. C'est de l'histoire élevée à la hauteur du roman!" I prefer good old-fashioned history, and confess to a weakness in believing it the better for age.

NOTE 27. PAGE 59.

" So with the moral frame—the man—who wore
Mind—matter, as a garment."

In the past tense, referring to the original state of creation, in which all that is animal was kept under subjection by the true immortal man. He was, before death by transgression, led and guided by the unerring Spirit of God. Mind and matter were then but a garment for his use,—illustrated by our Saviour in the instructive discourse to his disciples, which winds up by the exhortation to seek "first the kingdom of God and his righteousness: and all these things shall be added unto you."—*Matt. vi.* 25-33.

NOTE 28. PAGE 80.

" To Roman ears brute valor bore the name;
To Spartan, theft was glory, fraud was fame;
Athena's justice, vaunted to the sky,
Was but to shun the vilest treachery."

The illustration of the last line has been furnished in

Note 23. A city so renowned, which has given the world statesmen like Pericles and Themistocles, artists like Phidias, and teachers like Socrates, necessarily claimed the foremost place in civilization. Among the Romans virtue had reference chiefly to courage and martial accomplishments. Education with them was directed specially to the formation of the embryo soldier, but, with the Lacedæmonians, the birth, life, training, and sole end and object of the citizen was to make of him a perfect fighting machine. On entering the world, he was examined as to his qualifications, and, if rejected by the board of ancient men, cast into a deep cavern near mount Taygetus, to die miserably. If deemed worthy to enter the great republic, he was duly educated until sufficiently developed to fight for it, with every feeling and aspiration, and comfort and thought, sacrificed to the insane purpose of making his body the best and most available motive power for the weapons of steel he was destined to employ. His moral training is exhibited by the following quotations from Plutarch's Life of Lycurgus :—

"One of the best and ablest men in the city was, moreover, appointed inspector of the youth: and he gave the command of each company to the discreetest and most spirited of those called *Irens*. An *Iren* was one that had been two years out of the class of boys; a *Melliren* one of the oldest lads. This *Iren*, then a youth twenty years old, gives orders to those under his command, in their little battles, and has them to serve him at his house. He sends the oldest of them to fetch wood, and the younger to gather pot-herbs : these they steal where they can find them, either slyly getting into gardens, or else craftily and warily creeping to the common tables; but, if any one be caught, he is severely flogged for negligence or want of dexterity. They steal, too, whatever victuals they possibly can, ingeniously contriving to do it when persons are asleep, or keep but in-different watch. If they are discovered, they are punished not only with whipping, but with hunger. Indeed, their supper is but slender at all times, that, to fence against want, they may be forced to exercise their courage and address."

" The boys steal with so much caution, that one of them, having conveyed a young fox under his garment, suffered the creature to tear out his bowels with his teeth and claws, choosing rather to die than to be detected. Nor does this appear incredible, if we consider what their young men can endure to this day; for we have seen many of them expire under the lash at the altar of *Diana Orthia.*"

Treachery and cunning, thus taught in youth, produced a crafty and faithless people. This was shown by their conduct in the Messenian wars, wherein bribery of the Arcadian king and the Delphic oracle was freely used, as also by their horrible treatment of the Helots at home. If christianity tends to humanize and make saints of men, the Spartan institutions converted them into devils for the tor-ment of each other, and the destruction of all enjoyment in themselves. The greater their *virtue* in living out their principles, the more terrible the scourge to themselves and their fellow-men.

NOTE 29. PAGE 93.

" *On Horeb's brow the prophet stood,*
To hold communion with his God."

It was long after writing these that, for the first time, I was made aware of the fact that Campbell had commenced a piece on the same subject with precisely the same lines. I am satisfied that they were as originally developed, from the Scripture text, in my mind as in his, and although, to

11 *

avoid the charge of plagiarism, it would be easy enough to make a change. I prefer, with this explanation, to let them stand.

NOTE 30. PAGE 97.

" To whom thy virtue now, so rarely known,
Where dark intrigue pollutes a nation's throne ?"

The minor pieces in this volume were written at various periods as occasion suggested their composition. They, with the leading one, just finished, would probably never have been thus put forth, but for my earnest desire, amounting to a conviction of religious duty, to bear my testimony against Infidelity in its latest and most specious form. Until I had fairly seized this subject, the stanzas on Peace were more the recreation of leisure hours than written with a view to publication. The last in the series dates in 1854, on the Crimean war between Russia and the allied forces leagued to defend Turkey. That on Chief Justice Marshall, as it purports to have been, was composed in 1835, when he died. It was a period of great political excitement, and, in my judgment, the transition phase of the country from simplicity and integrity in the management of public affairs, to that of practically holding all the honors and emoluments of office as the spoils of victorious partizans. Those who remember the squabbles in the cabinet not long before, and the dismissal of our townsman, for his honesty and firmness, will scarcely think the above quoted lines too severe. I wish to be just to the living and the dead,—to faithfully depict the truth without trenching on private feelings, or unnecessarily introducing what may offend, even now after the lapse of so many years. My motto is, I trust, "principles, not men," and I have aimed to illustrate the former, with the wish to leave the latter to that Judge who alone can penetrate their motives to action.

THE

LIFE AND TIMES

OF

BERTRAND DU GUESCLIN.

A HISTORY OF THE FOURTEENTH CENTURY.

BY

D. F. JAMISON, OF SOUTH CAROLINA.

2 vols. 8vo.

THE DIVINE GOVERNMENT.

BY

SOUTHWOOD SMITH, M.D.,

Physician to the London Fever Hospital, and Medical Member of the General Board of Health; author of "The Philosophy of Health;" "The Common Nature of Epidemics," etc. etc. 8vo.

THE COMMON NATURE OF EPIDEMICS

And their relation to CLIMATE AND CIVILIZATION. Also, Remarks on CONTAGION AND QUARANTINE from writings and official reports.

BY SOUTHWOOD SMITH, M.D.,

Physician to the London Fever Hospital; Consulting Physician to the Hospital for Diseases of the Skin; Member of the General Board of Health, 1848—1854, etc. etc. Edited by T. BAKER, ESQ., of the Inner Temple, Barrister at Law, author of "The Laws Relating to Public Health, Sanitary, Medical, Protective," etc. etc. 1 vol. 12mo.

SKETCHES OF RUSSIAN LIFE

BEFORE AND DURING

THE EMANCIPATION OF THE SERFS.

EDITED BY

HENRY MORLEY,

Professor of English Literature in University College, London. 1 vol. 12mo.

INNER ROME:

POLITICAL, RELIGIOUS, AND SOCIAL.

BY THE

REV. C. M. BUTLER, D.D.,

Professor of Ecclesiastical History in the Divinity School, Philadelphia; author of "The Book of Common Prayer inter-
preted by its History;" "Lectures on the Apocalypse;" "St.
Paul in Rome," etc. etc. etc.   1 vol. 12mo. $1.75.

From the Philadelphia Inquirer.

. . . No modern volume within our knowledge has so thor-
oughly entered into an exposition of the government and the social
condition of Rome.

From the Cincinnati Gazette.

The book is the result of personal observation as well as the careful study of documents only made public since the surrender of the
Venitian capital to Victor Emmanuel.   Hence we find disclosures of
long permitted wrong, oppression, and cruelty, that startle us even
in this day when rebellion has given so bloody a record of crime.   It
is the duty of every man to read a volume so opportune, and which so
clearly indicates that the Old World is about to pass through an or-
deal more severe, if possible, than that in which our own land and
people have been tried, and, we trust, purified.   We commend the
volume to the student, the politician, and the practical man.

From the Rev. Dr. S. I. Prime.

. . . No book on Rome or Popery has met my eye so well fitted
to show the world what Romanism is at Rome, as this book of yours.

From Judge Advocate General Holt.

My dear sir: I write to thank you sincerely for the volume "Inner
Rome."   . . .   I have read it carefully and with much interest and
instruction, and think you have done your friends and the country a
good service in thus presenting to them the results of your diligent
study of the principles and policy and habits of those who have now
the guardianship of this "lone mother of dead empires."   Be assured
that I shall prize the offering alike for its own worth and as a token
of that friendship with which you have so constantly honored me,
and which I gladly and gratefully reciprocate.

From the Rev. Horatius Bonar, D.D.

My dear Dr. Butler: . . .   I am busy with your work, and find
it exceedingly interesting and instructive.   One likes to get a view of
the interior from one who knows it so well as you do; as for a trav-
eler, like myself, he is not qualified for the task at all, and his pen
can only sketch exteriors.   You have seen a great deal both of Rome
Inner and Rome Outer, and it is pleasant to be introduced by you
into one chamber, and another, and another.

GOLDEN TREASURY SERIES.

London edition. Uniformly printed in 18mo., with Vignette Titles by T. WOOLNER, W. HOLMAN HUNT, T. NOEL PATON, R.S.A., etc. In 15 vols. Price, $28.25, viz.:

A Book of Golden Deeds of All Lands and All Times.
Gathered and narrated anew by the author of "The Heir of Redclyffe." $1.75.

The Sunday Book of Poetry for the Young.
Selected and arranged by C. F. ALEXANDER, author of "Hymns for Little Children." $1.75.

The Book of Praise, from the Best English Hymn-Writers.
Selected and arranged by ROUNDELL PALMER. $1.75.

The Golden Treasury of the Best Songs and Lyrical Poems in the English Language.
Selected and arranged by F. T. PALGRAVE. $1.75.

The Children's Garland, from the Best Poets.
Selected and arranged by COVENTRY PATMORE. $1.75.

The Ballad Book. A Collection of the Choicest British Ballads.
Selected and arranged by WILLIAM ALLINGHAM. $1.75.

The Fairy Book. The Best Popular Fairy Stories.
Selected and rendered anew by the author of "John Halifax." $1.75.

The Jest Book. The Choicest Anecdotes and Sayings.
Selected and arranged by MARK LEMON. $1.75.

The Poems of Robert Burns.
Edited, with Prefatory Memoir, by ALEXANDER SMITH. 2 vols. $4.50.

Bacon's Essays and Colors of Good and Evil.
With Notes and Glossarial Index, by W. A. WRIGHT. $1.75.

The Song Book.
Words and Tunes selected and arranged by J. HULLAH. $2.25.

Pilgrim's Progress, from this World to that which is to come.
By JOHN BUNYAN. $1.75.

The Republic of Plato.
Translated into English, with an Analysis and Notes, by DAVID J. VAUGHAN, M A., and J. L. DAVIES, M.A. $2.25.

Robinson Crusoe.
Edited after the original edition by J. W. CLARKE, M.A., Fellow of Trinity College, Cambridge. $1.75.